Coates-Kinney

Mists of Fire

A trilogy and some eclogs

Coates-Kinney

Mists of Fire
A trilogy and some eclogs

ISBN/EAN: 9783337254513

Printed in Europe, USA, Canada, Australia, Japan

Cover: Foto ©Andreas Hilbeck / pixelio.de

More available books at **www.hansebooks.com**

MISTS OF FIRE

A Trilogy

AND SOME ECLOGS

By Coates Kinney

Chicago and New York:
RAND, McNALLY & CO., PUBLISHERS.
MDCCCXCIX.

CONTENTS.

MISTS OF FIRE.

SOME ECLOGS.

vi   CONTENTS.

    The apostrophè to an old appletree in "Mists of Fire" and the
poems "Singing Flame" and "Our Only Day" are from Harpers'
Magazine by permission.

MISTS OF FIRE.

A Trilogy.

——far

He whirled in mists of fire and knew that time
Would make his nebula stand forth a star.

p. 10.

————

KAPNISMA.

—— οὐρανὸν ἷκεν ἑλισσομένη περὶ καπνῷ.

Iliad I. 317.

I.

The south sun's molten beam of morning, poured
  Slant through my window, casts a golden bar
Along here by me, which I musing tow'rd
  Mottle with blue smoke blown from my cigar.

May sun in mid-November! and the purr
  Of one demure flame puttering in the grate
Is of the season sole remembrancer:
  Which is it, sun or flame, befits my state?

8   *MISTS OF FIRE.*

My state of age is as the waning year,
  But still my spirit seems yon sun of gold;
Nor can I make the thin flame lurking here
  Seem life's armed watch against the final cold.

Yet when I duly think I needs must know
  That this mistimed resplendence can not last;
Soon shall I cuddle to my firelight's glow,
  And only dream therein the radiant past.

Why, then, should I sit idly dreaming now?
  Wherefore not strive to seize the shining day
And ray it to a nimbus round my brow
  For pride and praise when I have passed away?

But pride in what, forsooth, and praise from whom?
  What could the plausive breath of millions be,
Or fame's procrastined flattery on a tomb,
  After the darkness has gone over me?

Yet, be it vanity or be it art
  Yearning for utterance, I seem to feel
A very Sinai thundering in my heart
  To make the multitude in worship kneel.

Not, surely, to exalt me as a name,
  But as a mandatary chosen of God:
Death on the hight at last with Him is fame,
  The good land spied whereto His people plod.

There is no glory worth a moment's thought
  Save that which links the memory of a man
To some fair order out of chaos wrought
  By him creating on creation's plan.

His work it is that lifts the human life:
  While others lead by law's and battle's might
He rises into calm above the strife
  And sets new guiding-stars along the night.

Though to the vision of his time and race
  Be only darkness where his far thoughts fly,
Yet; looking through himself, he well may trace
  The constellation men shall know him by.

How doubt that Shakespeare, measurer of worth,
  Gaged his own measure? Was that splendor dim
Which should outsplendor all the names of earth,
  Was that, now dazzling us, obscure to him?

Did he all realms of human thought explore
  And search all nature to its heart of fire,
Yet'his own majesty of man ignore
  In London playwright and in Stratford squire?

Nay, though he lavished radiance like the sun,
  He knew the world would roll round to his shine,
And sat serene to let the centuries run
  Till all their summits took his dawn divine.

He needed not his generation's praise
  For merit higher than their ken could prize,
Contented to forefeel the coming days
  When he should fill the more expanded skies.

So Browning: issuing from out sublime
  Regions beyond the measured cosmos, far
He whirled in mists of fire, and knew that time
  Would make his nebula stand forth a star.

But not so all; there are fine natures, new
  To this bleak oldness of the world, that need
The balm of bland south winds. and sun, and dew
  To fetch them into flower of word or deed.

Such see not in their dreams their destinies,
  But doubt, and woo sleep to confirm their
    dreams,
Turning from test of that which in them is
  To trust of that which round them only seems.

To them the Present's flattery is breath
  Of life, and by the fashion of the hour
And by the Past's rescriptive shibboleth
  They measure all the growing Future's power.

Their souls endeavor not against rebuff,
  But up the sunshine softly drift, and thin,
And vanish; as the smoke I gently puff
  Along the beam here past me slanting in.

Our sky is one vast empty bubble blown
  Full of such promise of forgotten men;—
Nay, them that are in streams of stars upflown,
  Millions of them, we never name again.

Yet these have fixed their glimmers; they shall last
  With those whose larger gleams the night be-
    gem;
They stand the steadfast presence of the past,
  And time forevermore looks up to them.

Even thus to give light, though no name of it
    Were known on earth, is glory worth the aim;
But O in forefront of the heavens to sit,
    A titled immortality of flame!

Call it ambition, call it worldly pride,
    Defiance of the faith, of wisdom scorn—
The soul's high sun-dream of life's other side,
    It is keen Phosphor looking to the morn.

It is a testimony, though a doubt:
    Our longing props our Heaven of prayer and
        song,
Yet we are loath to lose ourselves from out
    These wraiths of memory that to earth belong.

Were we as sure of that new life beyond
    As faith would keep us did we well believe,
Who would so closely hug this fleshly bond,
    Or to memorials here so fondly cleave?

What should the rapt souls in a world of bliss,
    From ardor there to heavenly ardor whirled,
Care for the little life they loved in this,
    Or for remembrance in this little world?

It is the feeble faith which supplicates,
  "Lord, I believe, help thou mine unbelief,"
That wavers in its claim to both estates,
  And dies contesting for the lower fief.

But is it lower? Why not instinct guess
  The evolution of the brain and give
Forecast of Universal Consciousness,
  Wherein all souls of all the past shall live?

What surer future can the Faith affirm
  For spirit than that All-Intelligence
Shall memorize itself from bloom to germ
  And trace its own growth back through every
    sense?

Since we are not to live hereafter by the flesh,
  But only by the spirit, what is that
Other than this life's memories to refresh
  In some new life, in some new habitat?

And if One Mind contains the universe
  As all-involving essence, it shall sum
Together these our memories and rehearse
  Them as One Memory in some world to come.

Man's rising in such Memory is the soul—
    This is the soul, or else the soul is not:
To be a mind so recollected whole
    Is life, as it is death to be forgot.

Not strange, then, is it that our nature strives,
    In spite of other faiths' imaginings,
To reach the hight of memorable lives
    With heavenward flutters of terrestrial wings.

The keenest pang of dying is the dread
    That ere our green graves' tiny billows sink
Back to the calm of some old churchyard's bed
    Men will have ceased to speak of us or think.

But, ah me, when the plowman drives his share
    Along the level sward above our sleep,
And, even of our oblivion unaware,
    Upturns our mold to sow therein and reap!

Shall we grow into food to feed our kind—
    Our grosser part their grosser nature build—
And yet our Substance, mind, from out the mind
    Of all Humanity be struck and killed?

Not so! As these my wafted breaths of smoke,
  Although they vanish, can not perish, thus
Not even Omnipotence has thunderstroke
  Potent enough to slay the souls of us.

This mind, even as this matter, element
  All indestructible though suffering strange
Vicissitudes, shall be forever blent
  With its Great Integer through every change.

Doubtless the souls of most must be but small,
  Since little lives give little to record;
But, lo, there doth not any sparrow fall
  Without the recognition of the Lord.

          *   *   *   *   *

Now suddenly, as here I muse and grope
  Amid the mysteries, I hear the quick
Sharp shocks of parting time's farewell to hope—
  Time dropping through my old clock tick by
    tick!

O time! time, miracle of mystery too!
  When life from full orb has begun to wane,
Like dreams that brush a baby's slumber through,
  The old years drowse and dwindle in the brain.

Between a thought and thought or act and act
  The longer, oftener oblivion gaps,
The more the circlings of the world contract;
  And time is not time in the interlapse.

Yet time, too, ends not when our reason dotes
  Amid the measured wheelings of the spheres;
Imperishable matter still connotes
  These massive motions which are days and years.

But think how, when the reckoning brain is gone
  Back to blind atoms of the earth and air—
Though yet these motions—how can time go on
  Without our sentiency of when and where!

Mere motions that the sleep of death have crossed
  Are not duration, and do not exist:
So myriads of ages might be lost
  Out of eternity and not be missed.

And that is solace. Though there intervene
  Eons on eons ere the dead awake,
A lightning's-flash shall be the time between
  The conscious life they leave and that they take.

Life is by atoms: when it has impinged
 On every atom of the cosmic mass
And all that Body with the Spirit tinged,
 Then Universal Soul has come to pass.

An atom that has lived can never lose
 The vital impress, but with kindred swarms,
In ways heredity or chance may choose,
 Must reassert its life in other forms.

Thus atoms that alive have livest force
 Are such as most their parentage reflect:
So shall at length they all declare their source
 And all their past revive and recollect.

They into forms of living reconstruct
 The past of matter, flesh and blood re-wrought;
Why should imagination, then, reluct
 At reconstruction of the past of thought?

Imagination! she must govern still:
 Creatrix of the sciences and faiths,
Our shimmering skies she fills with worlds at will,
 And skies beyond with paradise of wraiths.
 2

Shall she geometrize across abysms
  Between   stars—ay,   explore   the   stars   them-
    selves—
Yet here grope darkling in old mysticisms,
  Turning from seraphim to dance with elves?

Imagination, this consummate blowth
  Of all the faculties, once being rid
Of ignorance and superstition both,
  Shall search all secrets and all mazes thrid.

I hold that man shall sometime understand
  The origins from which his being sprung,
And know himself back to beginnings planned
  In Nature's matrix when herself was young.

Into his memory shall he, imaging
  Life's radial lines from his own center back,
So all precursors of his selfhood bring
  That they no attribute of soul shall lack.

Incredible? Impossible? Absurd?
  Smoke on the brain? But what stands farther off
From reason than the life, unseen, unheard,
  Which Faith avers, in spite of Reason's scoff.

Imagination to religion raised
  And out of clouds of old tradition flashed
Delivers thunder, and our reason dazed
  In reverence and marvel shrinks abashed.

But shall Imagination now forget
  Her faculty of miracles, and down
Before Reality's dull coronet
  Of bronze and iron cast her golden crown?

Nay! she is Iris, and the cloudy dark
  That science shuts against the heavenward eye
Of spirit she illumines with her arc
  Of colors caught from white light of the sky.

There is much more to know than Reason knows,
  Much more to find than Science yet has found;
And whither winged Imagination goes
  They well may follow, fluttering from the ground.

She is the Flying-Spirit, and her trust
  Is in the yet unknowable which yawns
In thought's blank skywardness; and soar she
      must
  There lark-wise into high and higher dawns.

And if she here has intimated truth,
    Shall these her utterances to mockery move
For that there is no proof of them, forsooth?
    The highest truths are those we can not prove.

Such mother thoughts may be as axioms
    To mathematics in that riper age
When mind through late-born intuition comes
    Into the fullness of its heritage.

Instinct of that it is within us burns
    As fever for more living and as thirst
To be more known and knowing, and that yearns
    To stand in man's regard as best and first.

The more we live, the more our living urge
    Upon the life around us, by so much
More nimbly shall our future selves emerge
    From atoms that have felt our vital touch.

And whosoever here has lived his best
    To others, by his mind in theirs expansed
And by their memory thus of him possessed,
    Is nigher unto risen soul advanced.

The golden rule of Christ, then, is engraved
  On nature's heart; to do our kind most good
Is most by their remembrance to be saved
  As spirit in their coming spirithood.

O selfish soul of me! the thought thou knowst
  As duty to the neighbor shall be warmed
With the quick comfort of the Holy Ghost,
  And heaven shall catch thee in the good per-
    formed.

But what is good?—grand question that has tasked
  All time's best wisdom, and yet rests involved
With 'What is truth?' the question Pilate asked
  Of Jesus, nor without it shall be solved.

Jesus was silent; let the Roman law
  Declare his answer from the Roman cross—
And ruled Rome, though his dying vision saw
  Round him the Caesar's brazen eagles toss.

His good was life that all men's hearts applaud,
  His truth was innocence' victorious death:
In three days both arose and walked abroad,
  To fill Rome and the world with Nazareth.

Disciples, clouds of witnesses, evince
  Their knowledge of him, how that still he stirs
Their life and lives in them; and millions since
  His death have gone to theirs his worshipers.

Men mark his sovereignty by spire and dome,
  And throne him in the skies with seraphim,
But when they seek aright his very home,
  In their own souls they find the soul of him.

The more men live the Christ, the more the Christ
  Shall grow to person in his Christendom;
The slow world, meager-virtued, many-viced,
  Shall yet at length roll to his kingdom come. .

He was the fair first-fruits of them that slept;
  And when all wake to him his prophecy
Shall be fulfilled on earth, his promise kept—
  Humanity shall be Christianity.

His second coming in the flesh is pang
  Of birth of freedom in the throes of war—
Peace whispered where mad revolutions rang,
  And question what mankind are living for.

His coming in all flesh is slow and hard;
  But nature works without despair or scorn:
Though sin resist it and though wrong retard,
  Christ surely shall again as Man be born—

As Man in all men one—all then redeemed
  To him—as Man that aye himself renews,
And not, as Simon son of Jonas dreamed,
  Deliverer from Rome and King of Jews;

Nor yet as apparition in the clouds
  With blare of trump and loud angelic cry
Along the heavens' arch, summoning the crowds
  Of quick and dead to judgment in the sky.

His life by many thousand years foretook
  The growth of men; who only now begin
To read the secrets of the sacred book
  The largeness of his soul was written in.

The childlike marvels which have made the half
  Of him in worship (leveled to the brain
Of child-folk) shall be winnowed out as chaff
  Is winnowed to the winds from golden grain.

And to and fro shall run and be increased
The truth which was himself; that shall be he
Whom all men, from the greatest to the least,
Shall feel and know; that all in all shall be.

II.

But what is goodness? Is it selfishness?
How vainly questioned! Duty understood
Waits outdoors in the snow and under stress
Of winds of winter, and I dream it good

Again here, in my fire's caressing hold,
To watch my fancies as in smoke they float
About my chamber's mellow glow of gold
Or stop and swirl, sucked up the chimney's
throat.

Too precious in the brain my life has grown;
And the left moments of it look so scarce and
small
That I no more can bear to see them sown
Like seed afield, lest they unfertile fall.

But who would save his life shall lose it! Yea,
   I know—the treasure that is buried gives
No increase—and I know there comes a day
   When each shall answer for the life he lives.

Yet so I love my world—this world of thought,
   This business of my dreams, this drowse in books
Over the lore of life the dead have taught—
   That all my selfhood shrinks from outward looks.

My selfhood, ay and selfishness, it is—
   The German Goethe's yearning to absorb
More life, without that Sungod's-thirst of his
   To drain the light from every starry orb.

The egotism of culture was his cult—
   Worship of self with others' sacrifice;
And can it be that such supreme result
   Commends the priest through whom the victim
      dies?

From Jesus down to Goethe—down or up!—
   Between the thought Semitic and the Greek,
The soul asks, shall compassion drink the cup,
   Or passion pour it for the lowly weak?

        *   *   *   *   *

Was that an answer that a night-wind spoke?
 From out the dark methought I heard a cry
Of human sorrow, and the very smoke
 Here seemed to shudder as the moan went by.

Was it the pity of the cruel night,
 Its wail of pity even for whom it slays?
And shall I snug here to the warmth and light,
 While misery in the cold and darkness prays?

Yet what do I amiss—wherein have sinned?
 Can I lift all the downtrod, all the frail
Save from temptation? Why dost, then, O wind,
 Embitter me with thy rebuking wail?

What can a single soldier on the field
 Of battle, in the din of drums and yell
Of onset, when the shocked battalions yield,
 Torn through with thunder-scath of shot and
  shell?

What blame if in the rout of foot and horse
 He save himself and tarry not to ease
The dying or fetch off a comrade's corse—
 What blame to him that for his life he flees?

So, in the horror round us—cries and groans—
  The weak struck down—the fight gone over
    them—
The cruel victors' shouts—the women's moans!—
  O night-wind, how should I the conflict stem?

Besides, does not our later science teach
  That by the havoc of the weak the strong
Are strengthened—that the fittest cannot reach
  And hold their right without such seeming
    wrong?

Behold the ravage of the carnivores!
  They torture one another and devour;
And instinct that the victim's pain ignores
  Is the sole warrant of their life and power.

Lift off the night wherever round the globe,
  What tragedies of violence unveiled!
Light up the seas and their abysses probe,
  Lo, slaughter sworded and huge murder mailed!

Nature is heartless. But if human will
  And human conscience raise not man above
Her tests, whence is it that 'Thou shalt not kill,'
  Or, 'Thou thy neighbor as thyself shalt love?'

The human will and conscience! worlds that wheel
  Around some Sun beyond our scheme of things:
Their orbits touch this nature, but reveal
  Not whence the higher gravitation springs.

We must not plead the instinct of the brute
  To justify the human soul in sin:
The darkness of the ground, which fats the root,
  Rules not the light the blossom rises in.

The law which pricked the fratricidal Cain
  To cry, 'Am I my brother's keeper?' damns
The slayer, nay condemns even him who fain
  Would shirk the Christ's injunction, 'Feed my
    lambs.'

What *is* this? Is it Evolution's law
  Of self for self? Then, that which I call Me
Feels supernatural attractions draw
  Toward a grander Self that is to be.

The more the human consciousness expands
  The more it thrills with others' pleasure, as
The more their pain it feels and understands,
  And thus takes more life to the life it has.

So self grows larger; for it is the life.
　　So self grows nobler with its range more wide.
Self still shall seek its own—its own in strife
　　By fellow-feeling to be magnified.

Each of the million million sparks that star
　　This darkness is a separate centered sun;
The Sun to rise shall overshine them far,
　　And mingle all their shinings in its one.

Through ways of selfishness all nature moves
　　Unto a destiny unknown and strange;
To this each selfhood runs along its grooves
　　Of circumstance in time and change.

Our very will is tethered to the ground.
　　We cannot fly. The air we breathe is fate.
The food that cherishes our life we found
　　Predestined here to appetite innate.

Free will! Free to be well, and good, and glad,
　　In bodies of born sin and sorrow cramped!
Free to be sane though we were fathered mad!
　　Free will! with shackles of tradition clamped!

It was my grandsire reaching from his grave
  That pulled me back to darkness when I willed
An utterance of light and was not brave
  Enough to word the thought with which I
  thrilled.

A million voices from ancestral tombs,
  A million forces round me in the air,
Control my nature, and a million looms
  Have woven this life-vesture which I wear.

I am obedient to all the powers
  Of universal being; for I go
Back to its roots, as forward to its flowers
  I shall, through all its bole and branches, grow.

Is will, then, naught? Nay; though it is a pull
  Against all gravity, it is a lift
Of all so much; and one will, dutiful,
  May even the center of attraction shift.

Giordano Bruno, in the flames at Rome,
  In Campo Fiora, that day ere the fire
Of Holy Inquisition burned him home
  To God, when with the awful Triune ire

Of Father, Son, and Holy Ghost the Church
  Had cursed him and now held before his eyes
The mocking crucifix, forsooth to search
  His conscience with that sign of sacrifice—

Giordano Bruno turned away his face
  And would not see the desecrated sign,
But rather on his eyeballs took the grace
  Of blasting flames—and saw the light divine.

He saw, or sees, or shall see; for no past,
  Present, or future comes for him between
That death-flash and the dawn which is at last
  To wake the Nolan with the Nazarene.

Was that will nothing? Nay! it jogged the world
  And fetched its pole back to the north-star.
    Now,
Where then her flames above his ashes whirled,
  St. Peter's to his monument must bow.

The rack, the scaffold, and the fire attest
  The martyr's weight against the world of man:
One will, truth-armed, may clip the tyrant's crest
  Or tame the thunders of the Vatican.

The Great Republic bred her free-born sons
  To smother conscience in the coward's hush,
And had to have a freedom-champion's
  Blood sprinkled in her face to make her blush.

One Will became a passion to avenge
  Her shame—a fury consecrate and weird,
As if the old religion of Stonehenge
  Amid our weakling worships re-appeared.

It was a drawn sword of Jehovah's wrath,
  Two-edged and flaming, waved back to a host
Of mighty shadows gathering on its path,
  Soon to emerge as soldiers, when the ghost

Of John Brown should the lines of battle form.
  When John Brown crossed the Nation's Rubi-
    con,
Him Freedom followed in the battle-storm,
  And John Brown's soul in song went marching
    on.

Though John Brown's body lay beneath the sod,
  His soul released the winds and loosed the flood:
The Nation wrought his will as hest of God,
  And her bloodguiltiness atoned with blood.

The world may censure and the world regret:
The present wrath becomes the future ruth;
For stern old History does not forget
The man who flings his life away for truth.

In the far time to come, when it shall irk
The schoolboy to recite our Presidents'
Dull line of memorabilia, John Brown's work
Shall thrill him through from all the elements.

Only his will is free that has been freed
From dread of death. That terror holds us bond.
We hoard the life here with a miser's greed,
Grudging to spend it for a life beyond.

Naught of his own whereon man sets his heart—
Love, fortune, honor, soul's or body's lust—
But he holds dreading when the fatal dart
Of death shall strike it from his grasp to dust.

And even though death, swift executioner,
Were welcome in our Pleasures' loss and lack,
The jailer Pain, deliberate minister
Of justice, whips us to our dungeon back.

3

As Faith dies, present losses, present gains,
  Make more and more the life ; and Science knows
No higher function yet than out of Pain's
  Thickset of thorns to pluck us Pleasure's rose.

O Science! yon expanse thou pushest out
  To where the cosmic suns are glimmers dim,
And must thou blot man's inner heaven with doubt,
  And dwarf the soul to this mere self of him?

Such dwindled soul as, though all else were damned,
  Would save itself and seek its own reward
Is what thou, Science, into brain hast crammed
  And left to end there by the doom abhorred.

But does the Faith conceive a larger soul?
  Nay, larger in duration, not in aim :
The bliss of self in Heaven she dreams as whole,
  With half mankind in everlasting flame.

Self, self, self ever, self as hunger, thirst,
  As greed of ownership, as center, sum
Of all desires, self seeking to be first
  Or best in this life or in life to come!

The Oriental fancy, in its dream
   Nirvana, whereinto the souls ascend,
Lets Lethe through their selfhoods flow and stream
   To cleanse them of beginning as of end.

That tenet of the Hindoo wisdom feels
   Toward the unutterable truth: the peace
Of God, round which the Western reason reels,
   Is the All-Self, wherein all selves shall cease.

All lines of selfishness converge to that,
   And all to one another draw more near
As all approach what each is aiming at—
   The center of the universal sphere.

Is this the doctrine of prosaic Pope—
   'Whatever is is right,' in rhythm and rhyme?
Not so; it is his logic lit with hope:
   There is no IS from point to point of time.

Right is a process; what to one blind age
   Is wrong that makes the wild mobs rave may
      mark
With a particular glory history's page
   And shine forth starlike from the general dark.

A straightening from errors and mishaps,
  Direction forward out of ignorance,
Right is a process; wrong a retrolapse—
  A gliding-back that measures right's advance.

The world that was created in six days
  Is yet creating. Man is Adam still,
And woman Eve, and still the serpent's ways
  Are poison, till mankind the doom fulfill

Upon it—trample underfoot and crush
  The lower, so to rise and meet the call
Of the Lord walking in the evening's hush
  And show no cringe of cowardice at all.

The tempting spirit in disguise that creeps
  Upon its belly, and that weaves its charm
Of dream's bewitchment and a lull like sleep's,
  Of wisdom known, shall lose its power to harm.

It is my faith that man shall yet receive,
  Even through the pains of sin and pangs of birth
And throes of death, the virtue to achieve
  The deed of immortality on earth.

Though this poor body shall not witness it,
   The tree of life, which has eternal growth
By evolution that is infinite,   '
   Must sometime come to amaranthine blowth.

And this my soul, though held long in the gloom
   Of the slow growth's expansion, shall not sink,
But, flushing upward, through that final bloom
   Shall taste the skies and wines of sunlight drink.

But, ah, the gloom! this darkness which shall yawn
   Between my day of life now soon to close
And that unspeakably far future dawn
   Which I must wait for in the dread repose!

The horror of it who is there that scapes
   In age?—sun setting, death's Pacific deep
Stretching out skyward from the western capes,
   And on the beach his little boat of sleep!

O, it is well the faculties are dulled
   By Nature in the old years! so the soul,
Within the wasting body soothed and lulled,
   Revolts not at her motherly control.

She slows the functions of the sense and dims
  The consciousness; with kisses calm, and mild
Caresses, and sweet memory's evening hymns
  She charms to sleep the worn and weary child.

But sad it is when still the spirit burns
  In old age clear and keen, and passions war
In the weak frame, and strong ambition yearns
  For years, and dreams jump to the Terror; for

In all life where is tragedy like that
Which acts its darkness in an old man's brain
When from the mystery sleep he wakes at night
And ponders on the greater mystery, death?

The phantoms of his years throng round his bed
(At first he knows them not from that night's
        dreams),
And he remembers each one as himself—
So many times himself a ghost in death.

So much of him already lived away!
From boyhood's age of flame, youth's day of fire,
Through manhood's hour of ardor, down to this—
A moment's flash between a sleep and death!

Ah! fair world rolling through the heaven of stars,
Its lands and seas, the thoughts and deeds of men,
The stir of nations, all to drop at once
Into the inane and dreamless night of death!

How shall these memories, these gains of man,
These treasured sweets of life, the gatherings
Of time so garnered in this flesh and blood,
Be flung down to the sudden waste of death?

O Death! thou art a far thought when the sun
On high is shining and the blood is quick,
While action roars around and busy days
Forget—thou art a far thought then, O Death!

But in the darkness, when the years are dreams,
When winds whine round the gables, wailing hope
As a lost spirit, then as near as life,
Nearer than madness, is the thought of death.

For such a sick old age there is no cure;
   Age needs the second childhood and the Mother's
      breast—
To Mother Nature snuggling for her pure
   Soul-solace through the twilight into rest.

If she sustain us not then, if she brood
  Not over us with palms in blessing crossed,
If she hush not our hunger-cries with food
  From her own fondling bosom, we are lost.

If so she do not mother us to calm
  Of babyhood at bedtime, then the joys
Of life in full play are the only balm
  For age's fever—give us back our toys!

Give to old Avarice his toy of pelf;
  To old Ambition statecraft, battlefield;
Give old Romance the rainbow's end, himself,
  And to old Glory give his lance and shield.

Old age that can not rest must neither rust;
  Rust eats the soul. Leave longings and regrets;
Look not before or after; what thou dost
  Do with the zeal which years and death forgets.

Blest such an old age when it has its forte
  In art or science, or in aught that brings
A use and need of studies that import
  Order and infinite imaginings.

This makes glad labor that is never done ;
   This charms the sundown with a glory's glow ;
'Follows the gleam' of heaven with Tennyson ;
   Flies with the strong old angel Angelo.

Old? Such rare spirits never age. We think
   Of their enlarged life but as youth increased :
So circumpolar June sun does not sink,
   But makes of utmost north both west and east.

And he is twice blest who in age pursues
   His art with young desire, but in the whiles
Of rest sits down with Nature and renews
   Himself to childhood in her mother-smiles.

This grim old appletree which many a May
   Has greened between my window and the morn
Seems to me thinking now in every spray
   A thought that is to be a blossom born.

Those maimed limbs plead thy story ;
   The wounds upon thy body speak for thee :
Thou art a veteran soldier scarred with glory,
   My brave old Appletree !

Oft hast thou borne up under
  Onset of storming wind and shot of hail;
And once a sword-lunge of assailant thunder
  Slashed down thy barken mail.

Old age, disease, and battle
  Have scathed and crooked and crippled all thy
    form,
And thy Briarean bare arms clash and rattle
  Tossed in the wintry storm.

I seem to feel thee shiver,
  As on thy nakedness hang rags of snow:
May charitable Spring, the gracious giver,
  O'er thee her mantle throw.

She will; and sunshine spilling
  From blue skies thou again shalt drink as wine,
To feel afresh the rush of young blood thrilling
  Through that old heart of thine.

For in the season duly
  Each year there rises youth's perennial power
Within thee, and thou then rejoicest newly
  In robes of leaf and flower.

Ay, though thy years are many
  And sorrows heavy, yet from winter's gloom
Thou issuest with the young trees, glad as any,
  As quick of green and bloom.

The bluebird, warbling mellow
  Refrains, like memory comes and calls thy name;
And like first love, the oriole's pomp of yellow
  Flits through thy shade a flame.

Thou quiverst in the sunny
  June mornings to the welcoming of song,
And bees about their business of the honey
  Whisper thee all day long.

Thus thou art blest and blessest—
  Thy grace of blossoms fruiting into gold;
And thus in touch with nature, thou possessest
  The art of growing old.

III.

As years increase, the wont of solitude
  Wins on the thinker—portals ear and eye
Shutting against the world, to interclude
  The common show and noise we know it by.

Pity for age when it grows garrulous
  With memories of the dead, and in eclipse
Of intellect gropes miserably thus
  To seek old friends in new companionships.

Rather smoke so alone amid the leaves
  Here where the moonshine flickers on the grass,
And feel the heavenly old remembered eves
  Like yonder westering star-streams overpass.

Nay, now the heavens fall round me, and their stars,
  These myriad fireflies, grow alive and near—
The far suns glimpsed in earthly avatars,
  Their years of motion flashed in instants here.

Fireflies thröugh the twilight glinting,
  How like memories they seem
Of the light of days departed—
  Little flying flames of dream!
So return the days departed,
  As the fireflies flit and gleam.

Fireflies, how like fleeting fancies—
  Come too thick for mind to mark,
Gone too quick for words to capture
  And withhold them from the dark;
Glimpses of that inner glory
  Never seen but spark by spark.

Fireflies, they are thoughts that ravel
  Mysteries to strands of light;
But the strands re-twist and tangle
  And go breaking off in night,
And the mysteries grow deeper
  As the ravelings grow bright.

Fireflies in the darkness twinkling,
  How like hopes of earthly things!
Hopes defeated, hopes repeated,
  Apparitions, vanishings:
Glancings of the Light Eternal
  Through a shadowy sense of wings.

Alone to heavens of memory—ay, and hells!
  Remorse unlocks the graves; deeds that have lain
Entombed so long that conscience hardly spells
  Their epitaphs arise again and reign.

But who or what shall help against the past?
  With bitter in the sweet I mixed the cup—
No chalice for communion! I, at last,
  Who poured it, I alone must drink it up.

What ear with mine could make this night-breeze
    moan
  Through living kissed lips that have long been
    dust?
Or in yon cricket's keen-cried monotone
  Hear that which fain my soul would not, but
    must?

Enough! I as the white light of a star
  By distance dwindled from a flaming sun
Would be beheld—flames, all that were and are,
  Into that gossamer of glitter spun.

There is no sympathy that I could bear.
  Say I have dreamed; but who shall enter sleep
To dream my dreams and their remembrance share?
  What a man sows, that let him also reap.

Omnipotence itself could not expunge
  Man's memory and save alive his soul;
He is by what he was before the plunge
  Into oblivion. Centuries to roll

Above his drownèd consciousness would grow
  Into eternity, did he not dawn
Like morning from the underworld, to glow
  In rays of self from rising memory drawn.

His weaknesses and passions, pains and sins
   Are parts of him no prayer shall pray away;
He may not blot from mind its origins,
   Nor in death's night sleep off life's yesterday.

The thoughts that are the Everlasting Fire,
   The thoughts that are the peace of Paradise,
Are not the sentence of the Day of Ire,
   Are not the purchase of Atonement's price;

They are the records on the tablets etched
   Of one's own soul by his own good and ill:
Out of our past the heaven and hell are fetched
   That shall together all our future fill.

Nay, this day is the day of judgment; this,
   This very eve of summer judges me—
Confounding my horizon's round of bliss
   With wrathful tossings of the nether sea.

Yet I am but a function of the cosmic life,
   A tool of nerves that nerveless Power employs
To work in matter: what to It my strife
   Of being—my small sorrows and my joys?

Name that Power God; is God, then, organism
  Of nerves, that pain and pleasure, life and death
Should touch Him—His white light, which this our
      prism
  Of sense in passion's colors pictureth?

There is no pain save in some ganglion
  Of nerves; to God, since he is absolute
Of such, our pains and pleasures are all one;
  For Him our suffering (this attribute

Of flesh and blood, our test of right and wrong)
  Is no criterion of what to do
In his wide cosmos; nerve and brain belong
  To Him as means to do His purpose through.

A thrill of least nerve-matter on a world
  (We call it pain or pleasure) is His touch
Shaping all worlds—an atom's atom's twirled
  Adjustment to a myriad million such.

Shall clay cry out against the potter's wheel
  That it is pain-pinched in the vessel's make?
Or to the potter that he does not feel
  The lump's endurance or the motion's ache?

Is God, so, concept of the fatalist—
Intelligence, and Will, and Predesign,
Creative Power no creature may resist,
Love that is infinite, and Wrath divine?

But why heap straw-pile logic Babel-wise,
Fire it atop with dream, and by the flame
Flashed into darkness hope to see the skies
Written across with letters of His name?

For here all thought how baffled, words how vain!
On tired wing out through regions measureless
Of suns and systems, suddenly the pain
Of our own littleness (the soul's duress

Of matter) strikes us like a rifle-shot,
And we fall fluttering to our world to gasp
The life out toward that Mystery we have not
Faculty even to dream a hope to grasp.

The Mystery of Godhood! Infant men
Have deemed it in their reach, as babes the moon:
God was Creator, next Destroyer, then
Redeemer, and to be Avenger soon.

4

But Pasht lies dead with Egypt's mummied cats,
  And Zeus is dumb in Hellas' marble art,
And Rome's Jove nods no more the Fate's fiats:
  The Man Christ having come, the gods depart.

"No eye hath seen the Father—who hath seen
  Me sees the Father": Jesus' paradox
To teach that form must ever intervene
  Between us and the Formless it inlocks.

The gods were finite when the world was flat,
  With low-hung stars for lamps that lighted it;
But science that the old Faith shuddered at
  Hath stretched the heavens and made God in-
    finite.

Whiteheat imagination into light
  And flash it straight a hundred million years,
Where is the sky it reaches in its flight
  That blazes not still on with swarming spheres?

Not strange that Rome should so have shrunk
    aghast
  From gazing through the Tuscan's telescope;
That startling revelation of the vast
  New awfulness of God blasphemed the pope.

For, face to face with these infinities,
  How dare define, or dogmatize, or prate
Familiarly of what God's person is,
  Measuring Him by human love and hate?

A gnat that lights upon my finger's tip
  As wisely might its thoughts of me rehearse
As I my fancies of acquaintanceship
  With the Live Unit of the universe.

Yet all the modes of reason men invent
  To solve the problem naught but growth shall
    solve
Are nature's means for mind's development,
  Are ways whereby all souls to One evolve.

We know God only as we grow to Him;
  To feel the Power, ourselves must be the Power:
The difference of men and seraphim
  Is growth from God in bud to God in flower.

                *   *   *   *   *

Lo, I have smoked the moon down! she has
    dropped
  Out of the midnight; and, as if all stir
Of thought had with her fallen glory stopped,
  My spirit lapses to a dreamy blur.

The darkness pushes and the shadows ramp
  On me, and seem to leave my soul no room:
I will within and by my study-lamp
  Labor for rest or think away my gloom.

*   *   *   *   *

ONEIRODE.

To think! to think and never rest from thinking!
  To feel this great globe flying through the sky
And reckon by the rising and the sinking
  Of stars how long to live, how soon to die!

This, this is life. Is life, then, worth the living?
  This plotting for his freedom by the slave!
This agony of loving and forgiving!
  This effort of the coward to be brave!

Our freedom! We are sin-scourged into being,
  And ills of birth enslave us all our days;
No chance of flying and no way of fleeing,
  Until the last chance and the end of ways.

We are walled in by darkness—wall behind us,
  From whose sprung dungeon-gates Fate dragged
    us in,
And wall before us, where Fate waits to bind us
  And thrust us out through swinging gates of sin.

But what is Fate?   It is a mere breath spoken,
  To echo clamoring between the walls
Of darkness—blind phrase uttered to betoken
  This blind Unreason which our life enthralls.

Out through abysmal depths of heaven around us
  We think our way past orbs of day and night,
Till skies of empty outer darkness bound us
  And place and time are fixed pin-points of light;

But nowhere from the silent planets wheeling,
  And nowhere from the thundering hells of suns,
And nowhere from the darkness comes revealing
  Itself a Fate that through all being runs.

No ghostly presence, no mysterious voices,
  The midnight of these infinite spaces thrill;
And even Chaos flies hence and rejoices
  To find and feel yon Universe's Will.

Thought follows chaos—nay, without the places
  And times of matter globed and motion whirled,
Thought chaos is, a spread dead wing in space is,
  Drifting for wafture somewhere toward a world.

Where shall it reach and touch the Will Universal?
  How with its confines bound the Infinite Mind?
One atom of the Allsoul's whole dispersal
  Assuming how the whole shall be defined!

Such thinkings are not Thought; they are but
    dreamings
  Of what perchance may be itself but dream:
Our truths are to the Truth as moonlight's gleam-
    ings
  In dungeon are to open noonday's beam.

All worlds of matter, all the world of spirit,
  How these are one, eternal, increate—
Soul can not clutch it, sense come never near it;
  It is unthinkable, and it is Fate!

This awful riddle, wherewith we have struggled
  Since the dim dawn of human consciousness,
With whatsoever dread words we have juggled—
  Ptah, Zeus, Jove, God—we fail, we fail to guess.

Whether there be of all intelligences
  A total Sum, a comprehending Whole—
Great sea, wherefrom rise all these mists, the senses,
  And back whereto flow all the streams of soul?

Whether this lives a selfexistent Essence,
  With its own passions, wills, imaginings,
Or is but everlasting evanescence,
  But perfume of the bloom of living things?

How cosmic spirit can take hold of matter
  And give dead elements the living breath?
How gather into selfhoods, and how scatter,
  To work the miracles of life and death?

Poets in grand imagination's trances
  Conceive the gods and give them wondrous birth,
And martyrs bleed for faith's divine romances,
  And priests go forth to proselyte the earth;

But what terrestrial religion reaches
  Out into heavenly majesty so far
That it may guess what god strange nature teaches
  To the strange dwellers on the nearest star?

Is Buddha known to denizens of Saturn?
  Is Jesus preached upon the Jovian moons?
And what are gods of any earthly pattern
  To far spheres drifting in the Force-monsoons?

Yon sun's flame, in whose light our worlds go dark-
    ling
  To eyes that from another system gaze—
Yon flaming sun is but a glimmer sparkling
  To like worlds blotted in the Dogstar's blaze.

And, howsoever gravitation labors,
  It lets a million suns from vision slip;
While the ten million systems are not neighbors
  Even by light's fine far swift fellowship.

How these immensities dwarf and obscure us!
  What, what are we amid such scenes as these?
Our Earth unguessed in planets of Arcturus,
  Undreamed in orbs around the Pleiades!

By such infinitudes of distance bounded
  (These chasms of darkness that no light can
    leap!),
We seem a dream with glooms of sleep surround-
    ed—
  Our life a dream surrounded with a sleep!

ANTONEIRODE.

Ay, we are dreamed; and if ever the Dreamer
  Wake from the sleep to remember the dream,
We of His waking shall thrill in the tremor,
  Dawn with His memory, mingle and stream.

What though He slumber through eon on eon?
  When He has dreamed all the infinite full,
Dreamed all the worlds and the lives there to be on,
  Out to dreamed gravity's uttermost pull;

Dreamed forth of matter and force interblended
  (Storm-drifts of matter and torrents of force)
Cyclones of flame, globed, exploded, and rended—
  Wide wild beginnings of Time's endless course;

Dreamed out of chaos the suns in the spaces,
  Dreamed down the suns to their white molten
    cores,
Dreamed off the worlds in their systemal places,
  Over them dreaming the continent-floors

Out of their pulps of fire—dreaming the oceans
  Out of the rain from their heavens of steam,
And of their mad elemental commotions
  Molding the motions of life in His dream;

Dreaming the marvelous atoms together
  Into the miracles feeling and thought,
Hitching, with matter's mysterious tether,
  Selfhoods of sense to insensible naught;

Dreaming the span of the measureless chasm
  Yawning between the alive and the dead—
Wonder of dreams in the organless plasm
  Crawling to soul from the sea's oozy bed—

Feeling to soul in the sea's vital foment,
  Feeling to form and to faculties dim,
Till, at the touch of a consummate moment,
  Loosed into freedom to rise and to swim—

Swimming of dreams in the nightmare of waters!
  Hydras, chimeras, and gorgons of sleep,
That by transitions of mutual slaughters
  Play the dream-tragedy Life in the deep;

When His long dream through the spawning and
      swarming
  Sea-generations has passed into things
Creeping aland, and has risen transforming
  Into the slow apparition of wings;

When from the budding of nerves in the banded
  Spirals of earth-crawling pleasure and pain
Upward has issued His dream and expanded
  Into the glorified blooming of brain—

Flower of all the world's forces and ages,
  Top-bloom of matter exhaling the soul,
Opening volume whose unopened pages
  Yet of God's being shall utter the whole,—

Here from His dream shall He start into waking—
  Dream of the universe waking in Me—
Me as a shore where the great billows breaking
  Leap out of silence in sounds of the sea!

Here, in the self of Me, here wakes the Dreamer,
  Wakes and shall wake as the brain shall unfold;
Here is the Christ of God, here the Redeemer,
  Spirit incarnate that Faith has foretold.

Growth of the brain shall be God manifested
  Here in the flesh, when the dead shall arise,
By an inherited memory vested
  With the immortal life dreamed of the skies.

Whatso has ever with being been gifted,
  Since the first givings of being began,
Living again shall be gathered and lifted
  In the Sovereign Consciousness, Man.

He shall remember all living and dying,
  He shall think back to life's origin here—
Nay, shall recall when he hither came flying,
  Seed of life ripened in some other sphere—

Brought by some inter-world wind accidental,
  Or by some gravity's fated monsoon,
Hence to be traced by that form rudimental
  Haply through all forms of life on the moon.

So shall he read the soul's mystery-story,
  Turning the pages from star back to star,
Now in the gloom and again in the glory,
  Till he shall come where the last secrets are.

Then, so with insight illumined to seeing
  All that has been, he shall see all that is—
Thrill with the pulses of all the world's being,
  Make all the God of the universe his.

Yet shall he, ere that divine consummation,
  All the career of existence have run,
World after world, to his last habitation—
  Seraph of light on the Ultimate Sun; ·

Sun, of the globes of all systems compacted,
  Orb, of all motion the center and rest
(Time to a moment eternal contracted),
  Goal of all spirits immortal and blest!

They shall be one, though their number be legion,
  And with One Consciousness they shall revive
Into the bliss of that radiant region
  All of the past that was ever alive.

PESSIM AND OPTIM.

PESSIM.

O this longing to live!
This tragical strife
Of us mortals to give
  Our lives more of life!

Give us new! give us more!
We hunger, we thirst,
We aspire, we implore—
  Give most, best or worst!

We inherit the ages
  Of human desire;
Ay, within us yet rages
  The older brute-fire.

All that is we have been,
  Of air, earth, or sea;
Whether wing, foot, or fin,
  One kindred are we.

In our blood flowing down
 From primitive man,
Savage, saint, sage, and clown
 Have blent as it ran.

All their lives are our life,
 Their lusts are our lust;
And we strive with their strife,
 Then—dust to their dust!

OPTIM.

Dust to dust?　No, that doom
 We will not endure!
Us the prisoning tomb
 Shall never immure!

When the star-stuff of heaven
 From God was outwhirled
It was stirred with the leaven
 Of life of the world.

PESSIM.

God? And where then was man?

OPTIM.

Lo, God and man one
Ere the fire-mist began
To swirl-in to sun!

For man's wills and desires
　　Repeat and rehearse
Those which motived the gyres
　　Of this universe.

Ay, and not only his,
　　But those of the whole
Life that was and that is
　　Of God, the One Soul.

Life eternally must
　　Be motion of Him—
From dull worms in the dust
　　To keen seraphim.

Every pleasure and pain,
　　Of stir in the clod
Or of thrill in the brain,
　　Is living of God.

5

Life shall vanish away
And finish its course
When He ceases to play
With matter and force.

PESSIM.

Will He cease?

OPTIM.

No, He never,
Till matter is hurled
Into naught, can dissever
Himself from the world.

All delights and all doles—
Thought, passion, and strife—
Are the Infinite Soul's
Large living of life.

PESSIM.

Then, on whom Faith has leaned
Lives not; for it seems
We are whims of some Fiend
That slumbers and dreams!

Unimaginable Demon!
　With cosmic fire-storms
In His crazed sleep to dream on
　And dream into forms!

Lo, a huge fancy runs
　Athwart His vast sleep,
And ten millions of suns
　Blaze out in the deep.

His deliriums dim
　In meteors flock,
And with whimseys of Him
　Wild stars intershock.

All the rocks are one tomb
　Of moods of His mind,
Cast away to make room
　For us living kind;

Phantoms! dancing and hymning,
　While here where we dwell
Is but film overswimming
　An ocean of hell!

Smoking peaks burst in thunder
And shower down death,
And the plains gape asunder
With doom in a breath.

Commerce rises and dips
With east and west sun,
As her shuttles, the ships,
Weave states into one;

But the sea, the brute sea,
That swings round the sphere,
Never heeds the wild plea
Of man in his fear:

Him and his its rude surges
Toss, buffet, and drown,
As it yawns in its gurges
And ravins them down.

And the beasts of the deep,
Like phantoms that form
In the nightmares of sleep—
Grim monsters that swarm

In the darkness of waters,
  And gorge mouth and maw
With their mutual slaughters
  By snout, tooth, and jaw—

How the swift silent beasts
  In combat partake
Of the fattening feasts
  The mad billows make!

'Lord of life and of death,
  Have mercy on me!'
Cry that squanders the breath
  On storm, night, and sea.

Cry for God's mercy where,
  In maniac bout
With the powers of the air,
  The great waters shout?

Where from mountains' pent hollows
  Hell bursts out on men?
Where earth opens and swallows
  And closes again?

Cry for mercy where thunder
　Drops death from the clouds?
Where the ghosts rise from under
　And mix with the crowds

Of the living, unheard,
　Unseen, and unknown,
Till with mortal plague stirred
　The scared cities groan?

Mercy! No, there is none
　In whatever force
Wherewithal the Lord Sun
　Gives life and death source.

'Fire!' A cry in the night—
　One cry, and no more
Ere the streets fill with fright
　And clamor and roar.

To the flames all the city!
　Stop not now to call
That Almighty have pity—
　The water has all.

'O my husband!—my child!'
 A mother and wife
In the first terror wild
 Has fled for her life

From the room where she kept
 Love's wake by dead love,
And her innocent slept
 Unfathered above.

'Dead!—dear love!' Off she flings
 Whoever delays
Her mad purpose, and springs
 Back into the blaze.

Through the flame and the smoke,
 Past him lying dead,
Up the stair, scorch and choke,
 To find the babe's bed!

Scarce a moment to speak
 One vain phrase of prayer
Ere the woman's death-shriek,
 And, framed in the glare

Through the window revealed,
    A picture that robbed
Men of breath, and down kneeled
    The women and sobbed;

Picture, flashed upon flame,
    Of two forms in white!
Then picture and frame
    One red blur of night!

Was it rage, was it ire
    Of some god above?
Or, mad hunger of fire
    For woman's mad love?

Woman's love! Love belongs
    To Force, and is part
Of the rights and the wrongs
    Of dull Nature's heart.

How is Force when it burns
    And flares out its breath
Worse than Force when it yearns
    And dares unto death?

What *is* better or worse,
　Where all only seems?
What is blessing or curse,
　In drama of dreams?

What is saintship or sin?
　To climb or to fall,
Or to lose or to win?
　The One lives it all.

'All delights and all doles—
　Thought, passion, and strife—
Are the Infinite Soul's
　Large living of life!'

Is it living of thought
　Or living of trance?
And is purpose outwrought
　From chance upon chance?

What purpose in killing
　My darling, my boy?
What demoniac thrilling
　Of infinite joy

From the little life lying
    In fever's hot flame
And in last anguish crying
    The mother's fond name?

Stricken wife of my youth!
    O, how from that day
Didst thou pine for what truth
    Death's morrow might say!

In the hope of that morrow,
    Thou, patient and brave
With thy burden of sorrow,
    Soon went to the grave

In the travail of mother
    Of that little-one
Who should follow the brother
    Ere one year were done.

O, the faint pulses' warning!
    O, loving last words!
In the spring, in the morning,
    With songs of the birds!

I explore all the dark,
  I search sleep for her;
But there comes not a spark,
  Or whisper, or stir

From all hearing, all seeing,
  All feeling of Force,
Hinting whether her being
  Hold conscious its course,

So that still might be shown
  Her dear form and face
And herself still be known
  In time and in space.

As the rose, as the lily,
  Yield up scent and hue,
Yield their ghosts to the chilly
  White death of the dew,

Did my home's living flowers
  So fade and exhale?
And have these lives of ours
  No other avail

Than to feel, love, and think
One moment of light,
And then suddenly sink
In morningless night?

Is existence too rife
In earth's human hives,
That the Life of all life
Should so lavish lives?

Lives of men, lives of brutes,
They crowd to their tombs,
Like the leaves, like the fruits.
Which fall for new blooms.

OPTIM.

Famine, pestilence, flood,
Fire, thunder, and quakes
Of the earth, and the blood
Volcanic that breaks

From the hot veins of mountains,
And tempests that plow
The great deep to its fountains—
Does God, thinkest thou,

Heed of thee in thy plaint
That these never choose
Between sinner and saint
Where life is to lose?

Holy Jews, ye that priced
God's life, and decried
The immaculate Christ,
And him crucified;

Ye, with credos for charters
To hunt and to slay,
That re-sainted with martyrs
Bartholomew's day;

Ye that bloodied the ages
With myriad lives' loss
In religion's blind rages
Of Crescent and Cross;

Ye that fire martial leaders
With adulant breath,
Making mothers proud breeders
Of doers of death—

All the civilizations
  Of man standing armed,
Nation fronting each nation's
  Blood-hunger, alarmed,—

How would dare ye appeal
  To God that He make
The brute elements feel
  For your human sake?

God is you and in you,
  As they and in them;
And shall one of His two
  The other condemn?

PESSIM.

Where is fault, then, or sin
  In them or in us—
We and all we are in
  Unpurposed as thus?

For be all forms and motions
  Divine, and they seem
But the miscreate notions
  Of God in a dream.

OPTIM.

No! the seeming is thine;
    For, could all the mass
Of the universe shine
    Through thy little glass;

Could the Allbeing flow
    Entire into thee,
So that Substance might show
    And Essence might see;

Couldst thou know what beginning
    To what end belongs;
Couldst thou witness Fate spinning
    The Right out of wrongs,—

Thou wouldst rise from the dark
    Wherein flesh is born,
And with song like the lark
    Soar into the morn.

No! the dreaming is ours;
    God's life is not trance,
But the sum of the powers
    Of all lives' advance.

How we struggle to live!
God urges the strife
Of all beings to give
Their lives more of life.

From the instinct that lurked
In plasm of old seas
He and we have upworked
Through myriad degrees,

Climbing higher and higher,
With gain upon gain,
Till at last the soul's fire
Is lit in the brain.

In this upward progression
Humanity's birth
Is the highest expression
Of God on the earth.

Yet the heavens are swarmed
With worlds older far;
And what lives, angel-formed,
May people a star,

Neither spectroscope's feel
  Nor telescope's ken
Shall avail to reveal
  To senses of men.

But these five senses grew,
  As others may grow—
Senses so searching-through,
  Brain facultied so,

Seized of force by such arts,
  That mind may embrace
Other mind in far parts
  Of infinite space.

Other mind may be there
  With powers so strange
That our own would not dare
  Imagine their range.

Can these pinholes of sight
  Of ours comprehend
With what uses of light
  High beings may send

The quick soul through the dense
    Vast darkness of naught,
And by some inner sense
    See us and our thought?

And to what fuller blowth
    This flesh shall unfold,
What the grandeur of growth
    Its energies hold,

Man can now no more dream
    Than through his life dim
In the worm there could stream
    A prescience of him.

But we know that we climb;
    We see that we rise—
See how time unto time
    We widen the skies.

From the ten fingers' count
    Of numbers, begun
In the savage, we mount
    And measure the sun.

Fabled Jupiter's nods,
  That Nature obeyed,
And those gorgonish gods,
  Her forces, which played

Chiefest part in mankind's
  Last dream before day—
All the myths from all minds
  Have faded away,

Where the Self-Revelator
  Immanuel stands
As the human creator
  By human love's hands.

God is with us and in us
  (Within is above),
And our lives work to win us
  His life by our love.

Whether I will or whether
  Will not as He would,
All with all things together
  Work only for good.

All the wrong I commit,
   Mankind so unite
To exterminate it
   They strengthen all right.

So, we grow by our sins;
   Iscariot betrays,
And the Nazarene wins
   Through all after days.

Lo, the Wrong that hath died
   To Hades is hurled,
While the Right, crucified,
   Redeemeth the world.

PESSIM.

But redemption to *come*!
   What boots that to thee,
Thou for eons then dumb,
   Deaf, dead soul of me?

What is this we have dreamed?
   Whereto have we raved?
When the world is redeemed
   Shall my soul be saved?

OPTIM

Timid soul! thou art fleeing
  False danger: fear not;
For thy sweet self of being
  Shall ne'er be forgot.

Man inherits the ages,
  And shall, with the whole
Of his grand heritages,
  Inherit the soul.

There are times when far places,
  Where strangers we roam,
Flash familiar with traces
  Of some former home.

There are hours when such trances
  Efface all that is
That we dream circumstances
  Of past centuries.

There are moments we hear
  A dead father's tone
In our voices, so clear
  It startles our own.

We are writ in as books
　By hands from the skies,
And ghost-ancestry looks
　Oft out of our eyes.

These are half-resurrections
　Of souls that are gone—
Dim and fitful projections
　Of that coming dawn

Of All-Consciousness, when
　In Man there shall stand
The whole lives of past men,
　So livingly scanned,

So remembered, so real,
　So self-substantive,
That, no longer ideal,
　They truly shall live.

Why is this a hard saying?
　Heredity grows,
And the part it is playing
　Shall never have close.

As the form and the feature,
　　The tone and the trait,
The whole self of each creature,
　　Are so destinate

From the procreant mold,
　　Shall mind not progress
Till by heirship it hold
　　All past consciousness?

And, if far-future Man
　　Remember so me,
From the hour I began
　　Till ceasing to be—

So revive me, so live me,
　　So breathe my soul's breath—
What is that but to give me
　　Sure triumph o'er death?

O immortal my soul!
　　To live and to know
And flow on with the whole
　　Divine Being's flow!

O my soul! from the dark
Wherein flesh is born
Soar and sing like the lark!
For here is the morn!

A KEEN SWIFT SPIRIT.

I.

Beyond these worlds of living and of dying,
  Beyond the sun, beyond the Pleiads seven,
A keen swift spirit of the Earth went flying
  Along outside the crystal walls of Heaven.

Never a soul had come to those walls younger
  Not bidden thither by the angel Death;
Never a mortal with diviner hunger
  For life above the life of blood and breath.

He was a youth grown old with love and sorrow,
  With wrongs of circumstance and faults of birth—
The grub Today with butterfly Tomorrow
  Aching within it as it crawls the earth.

His hopes were fire, and his imagination
  Flew forth as flame, to burn the world with them
And re-create the old stuff of creation
  For the Divine John's New Jerusalem.

But the dull world had deemed him scarce worth
    scorning;
His thought just bubbled on thought's ocean-
    stream;
And so his life had mooned away its morning,
    A blind sleep-walking in a fevered dream.

Now he had left himself here standing under
    The stars—so do the stars rare souls entice—
While he had flown out on the wings of wonder
    And stopped against the walls of Paradise.

He sought along and up and down for casement,
    Or gate, or loophole in those walls, but found
No entrance, and he drooped in such abasement
    That he fell back to flesh and clutched the ground.

And whether in the body then or whether
    Without the body, such a voice he caught
As of two flutes that sing at night together
    Into a dreamer's ear unearthly thought:

        The gates into peace are withholden
            To seeking of mortal sense,
        And never the Kingdom of Heaven
            Is taken by violence.

Man finds but the one gate of entrance—
It yields to the passer's breath
On hinges that give only inward—
The gate of the way of death.

But outward the secret gates many
Let open from bliss within,
Swing open for issuing angels
To pass to the worlds of sin.

As I with associable seraphs
That chorally sing and fly
Came out to the straight gate of Lyra,
Thy ardor I felt go by.

The virtue I felt of thy ardor
Go by like a whirl of fire,
And burned to upbear thee and steady
The flight of thy fierce desire.

I rushed to the gate and outpushing
I followed and fell with thee;—
But thou shalt arise again thither,
If thou wilt but follow me.

He started—lo, the stars above him gleaming!
  Upon his lifted forehead damps of dew;
And he grew ware that he had stood there dreaming
  While past him notelessly the winged hours flew.

But had he dreamed? No, no, that voice was real!
  He looked round for the angel's fleshly guise,
And met a maid's face that was love's ideal,
  Unutterable passion in her eyes.

She rose there in the moonrise like a lily—
  As if a lily that had sprung and grown
From the sown moonlight suddenly and stilly
  And into bloom miraculously blown.

"Sweet! O my darling!" cried he, arms outstretch-
      ing,
  "Hast thou come back to me here out of death?
And no reproaches in those fond eyes fetching!
  Nothing but love in them, Elizabeth!"

So cried he, running forward to infold her,
  Once more to fold the dear form in his clasp,
But when he reached his hand to grasp and hold her,
  A moonbeam through the pine-leaves mocked his
      grasp.

"I heard a spirit speak, as I am living!
If I stand here, I saw that form and face!"
And at his own shocked voice a shudder giving,
  He turned and fled as from a haunted place.

A sudden gust of childhood's superstitions
  Blew though his memory, and, as he sped,
A darkling company of apparitions
  Chased him with ghostly whispers of the dead.

He passed the old church with the graves around it;
  It seemed that all the white stones were astir!
And hers—how oft by day his flowers had crowned
    it—
Why should he flee in horror now from her?

But he paused not to chide his soul affrighted
  (Death's world was back of him and life's before)
Until he stood within his chamber lighted
  And had against the night locked fast the door.

"O Jesus! dear Redeemer!" sinking, kneeling,
  He prayed, "if I had stayed myself on thee,
I might have felt the other world with feeling
  Such as bestead thee in Gethsemanè.

"Yet, my Lord Christ! remember, O! recall thee
  That thou wast master over death and hell,
And nothing, as thou knewest, could befall thee,
  Even though Roman scourge and cross befell.

"But I am young and weak, and grope in error;
  Forgive me that thy courage could not save
My spirit from the lifelong world-old terror
  Of musing in the darkness on the grave!

"Sweet Savior! life is dear and light is glorious
  To the young man—O, give me life and light!
Life that is light and light that is victorious
  Over the awful powers of the night!"

II.

Years came to him, though never had come answer
  To that night's cry to Christ to make him whole;
But doubt had grown upon him like a cancer,
  Still eating toward the vitals of his soul.

He stumbled through the years, and as he stumbled,
  Men said he sinned against the Holy Ghost's
Longsuffrance, for that he had never humbled
  Himself to magnify the Lord of Hosts.

Life had he asked, not hope of life in Glory;
  Light had he prayed for, not for faith to stand
On Dogma's little island-promontory
  And feel across the blinding seas to land.

And, what though sky-roofed science all achieving,
  He longed beyond the far horizon's rim;
He raged to know; he could not rest believing;
  The mysteries of God were pangs in him.

For, what saith science of the great Beginning?
  A Force, however named (how empty names!),
Set infinite chaos thrilling, stirring, spinning,
  Till Darkness bloomed to countless million
  flames.

What was that Force—ay, what still is it?
  Those flames are suns, to globes is chaos whirled,
And life upon them comes a sudden visit
  From some unthinkable rare inner world.

O Life! Life first, life last, and life amiddle
  Of the eternity beyond the years
Of stars in motion! Whoso reads this riddle
  Shall hear the soundless music of the spheres.

Of this what teaches Darwin more than Moses?
Nor growth nor quick creation from the clod
Explains for us the blooming of the roses—
One least sweet secret of the life of God.

'There is no God'—the flippant fool's old saying,
The blinkard's logic, or the coward's curse!
What, then, this procreant Life-Force intraplaying
Throughout the matter of the universe?

I Am! The Hebrew seer's clairvoyant seeing
Flashed to the depths in that one fulgent phrase:
I Am—the Consciousness! I Am—the Being!
Whatever comes or goes, I Am—that stays!

I Am—in all things! and whenever, thinking,
Mind so forth-stars its being as to find
Its own form I-am, then begins it drinking
The influx of the Omnisplendent Mind.

Life's organ is a vase that death shall shatter,
And so, saith science, death shall Me undo.
What, then, is that which organizes matter
To form the vase and pours me thereinto?

Ay, what is that? The One Life Everlasting!
And that small part of it to me which runs,
Needing to fear no loss, and no outcasting,
And no undoing, shall outlive the suns.

But what becomes, thus, of the narrow teaching
That man alone to life immortal springs?
This thought of immortality is reaching
Enough to gather all organic things.

Organic, ay, as also inorganic,
In some mode must eternally survive;
But life is not life's energy mechanic—
Life's consciousness is all that is alive.

And though we needs must fail in our endeavor
To trace this in the dumb life downward, yet
Wherever life is *I* it lives forever;
I am I-Am, that never can forget.

Selfhood is first the little airy trouble
In depths of water—to expand and rise
Through clear and clearer, and at last to bubble
Out into God and with Him fill the skies.
7

God's play in matter is to man existence,
  Ay, and to all lower and all higher forms—
As low as in the sea-ooze find subsistence,
  As high as wherewithal the ether swarms.

For higher there are—man may not bear to hear it,
  As boasting God's own image—higher there are;
God's image is not frame of flesh, but spirit:
  I AM *I-am* in strange forms on a star.

This flesh-and-blood is so below our wishes—
  Our dreams as man, our childhood's reach of
    words—
We grudge their grace of swimming to the fishes,
  Envy the joy of flying in the birds.

And our desires are prophecies; as surely
  As sometime somewhere we shall live again,
So shall our lives be not our memories purely,
  But all our prayers shall live their full amen.

Religion notes this in transcendent features
  Of angels, and Apocalyptic John
Dreams truth in strange-formed, strange-eyed won-
    drous creatures
  With God's high glory clothed upon.

Who knows the outcome of life's evolution
  Even on planets that our sun reflect?
Mayhap rare winged shapes, with no diminution,
  But increase rather, of man's intellect.

Why may there not be souls of such high pattern
  In bodies of such superhuman mold
On moons of Jupiter or rings of Saturn
  That man in them would seeming gods behold?

And if, light's miracle of motion working,
  Natives of higher spheres could visit man,
What strangers might we greet from great worlds
    lurking
  Within the sun-blaze of Aldebaran!

If they could visit man! O, to unravel
  These mysteries of force which interlock
Planets and suns!—perceive how light can travel
  A million miles in six beats of the clock!—

How gravitation holds the worlds together,
  By atoms hitched, with air-threads dreamed of
    steel,
And reels the comets in with spun-out tether
  From distances the mind is dumb to feel!—

How panting pulse of heat through ether oozes
    Velocities that mock the lightning's flash,
And how the spirit of the lightning loses
    Its mighty silence in the thunder's crash!

To penetrate such secrets to their sources
    And essences would help us comprehend
How instant-constant Everlasting Force is
    To thrill the universe from end to end.

And through that Force, by impress hypnotismal
    Controlling sense and reason under sleep,
High souls may yet the intervoids abysmal
    Between the worlds with converse overleap.

Nay now, to such souls, may not worlds be blended
    And held in thought too fine for words to frame,
Even as some sun-system vast and splendid
    Is blent to vision in a drop of flame?

Doubtless; and these unspeakable thought-trances
    Of genius and rapt faith's foretastes of bliss
May be but glimpses of mind's high advances
    In ampler being, flashed back into this.

What though, then, dies this organ of the senses,
  The contents are not spilled when breaks the cup ;
The other world's divine intelligences
  Shall drink this consciousness and memory up.

III.

So he the ancient powers of darkness routed ;
  So he with death's keen terrors ended strife ;
No more now he believed, no more he doubted ;
  He knew that we have everlasting life.

Not such life, truly, as the resurrection
  Of this gross body promises to creed ;
Not life that is of flesh a mere affection,
  But life that makes flesh live, the life indeed.

"To know myself as Me and not another,
  In whatsoever form I may reside—
Whatever strange new nature Me may mother—
  This is the life indeed, this shall abide.

"O life !—but I would jump the inter-world abysses
  Now, in the flesh ! would slip the earthly bond
Now, ere my death, to find what this life misses
  In beatific spheres of life beyond.

"O life! O love! since death disbloomed my pleasure
  Of living, never has it ceased to seem
That love the space between the worlds must meas-
  ure
  And lead life over on a bridge of dream.

"Nay, she has measured it, and she has thrilled it
  With her sweet presence ofttimes; and I pine
To cross that bridge with her, if love can build it—
  Love, architect and pontifex divine!

"Since that night when the angel, from those bliss-
  ful
  Abodes I then believed in, sang her song
Between worlds, that world has been filling this full
  Of her felt constancy and yearning strong.

"She was that angel; and if I distorted
  Or heard not rightly what she sought to say,
It was that faith's traditions in me thwarted
  Her thought and warped her utterance away.

"But now I dawn to truth: she hath inspired me
  To seek her love in passion other far;
I am to find her soul; she hath desired me
  To meet her passion in a higher star.

"For still she loves; her fond eyes burn within me,
  And in my sleep she hugs me in her arms;
Her kisses in the night from sorrow win me
  And from the sinful day's delusive charms.

"Glad sleep!—I go to it as I went trysting
  In our first love; I lapse from life forlorn
And meet a dream from over-shadows misting
  Into her form, to mate with me till morn.

"We walk the world and live the old love over;
  We list love's whispers in the leafy darks;
Through meads we hunt love's luck in four-leaved
    clover,
  And taste the love-screams of the meadowlarks.

"What never in the mornlight or the noonlight
  Her tongue-tied bashfulness would dare let slip
She smiles to hear the brook tell in the moonlight
  And ripples babble it from lip to lip.

"And when at such times oft I make her sing me
  In right words what the ripples say in runes
She croons me sweets that hit my soul and sting me,
  Her rapt face glowing like the harvest-moon's:

Love's feet! we feel them on the brink
Along where we run crinkling.
Love's eyes! all four of them! we wink
The stars to watch them twinkling.
Love's thought! Love must be daft to think
We would not tell it tinkling.

Love's hair! but which head should possess
The short or longer tresses
Of heads together, who may guess?
Love's kiss—hah, love's caresses!
Not quite so cold as when we press
The chilly watercresses.

Ah Love! delicious little imp!
Almost enough to wimple
Us back up stream and into gimp
Of ice our wavelets crimple!
So might we teach thee to be primp,
Demure in every dimple.

But, Love, we may not stop: we sing
Ourselves on down the dingle;
And as we go our lives we fling
Together more and mingle;
But, ah warm hearts that closer cling!
Ah pulses warm that tingle!

"So she interprets me the ripples' voices;
She witches me, she kisses me, she brings
All moods of love to me, and she rejoices
My heart with passion's heavenward-flaming
wings.

"But sometimes, with sobbed stammerings, fierce
flushes
Of jealousy, and blinding tears, she lets
The dream ebb out, and sudden darkness rushes
Back on my soul, a surge of wild regrets."

IV.

The constant angel of his dreams in vision
Of soul's reality he hoped to meet,
Either in this or in some world elysian,
Ere yet his years of mortal were complete.

He sought some clew in ologies and isms;
Psychology, and hypnotism, and those—
How name them?—those material cataclysms
Of spirit which arrive in shocks and blows.

Once, in a circle that for spirits waited,
　A Lady took him with her wondrous eyes—
Weird eyes, that marvelously fascinated
　His thoughts, and seemed their secrets to surprise.

Those magic eyes went through and through him
　　blazing,
　And then withdrew and inward seemed to look,
While words she murmured, all his reason dazing,
　Came quoted from his heart as from a book:

　　"As I with associable angels
　　　That chorally sing and fly
　　Came out to the strait gate of Lyra,
　　　Thy ardor I felt go by.

　　"The virtue I felt of thy ardor
　　　Go by like a whirl of fire,
　　And burned to upbear thee and steady .
　　　The flight of thy fierce desire."

The circle their congratulations clamored,
　And pressed him to identify and name
The dead.　With horror he denying stammered,
　And lied the truth with love's courageous shame.

If ever falsehood needed no forgiving,
  Having no sin, it was that truth in mask;
For surely she was not dead, but most living—
  What life, they would not know how even to ask.

The dead live not as old forms resurrected
  In like new forms of unsubstantial air;
They live as facts of consciousness collected
  Into brain's living here or otherwhere.

And if an earthly life is not worth keeping
  Here in remembrance, elsewhere it is not;
Such life shall sleep, shall long continue sleeping—
  Though at the last it shall not be forgot.

It dies not, but shall sleep, and, when the waking
  Of Mind's all-consciousness has memorized
The universe, shall then come forth retaking
  The selfhood which had seemed so sacrificed.

What though oblivion drown it in an ocean
  Of weltering eons, when it shall emerge,
Without a memory of a dream of motion,
  The time will seem a second's oversurge.

But souls that soar, fine spirits that refresh us,
  And that renew the life their living graced—
These do not die; their being is too precious
  To lie an instant in suspension's waste.

These are caught up : by process of inclusion
  The larger mind of high worlds takes the less ;
Which has not died—it is not death, but fusion
  Of less with larger, eager to possess.

And naught of consciousness—life's very essence—
  In that containing mind shall this mind miss ;
For, by the two selves' inmost coalescence,
  That shall remember when it lived as this.

A noble poet of our time, in query
  On this rare theme of life in Life absorbed,
Has dreamed it as a state of blankness dreary,
  The memory blotted and the self unorbed.

What, then, is memory? Is it brain's possession
  Alone, to lapse with dying brain's release?
Or is it Life lived here in brain's impression,
  To hold in higher life when this shall cease?

And what is selfhood but in memory's mirror
  The living image of the life's own past?
That image, surely, shall be fuller, clearer,
  When in a larger, truer memory glassed.

But can there be brain capable of holding
  More than one memory—one life, that is?
Nay, why not brain a million lives infolding,
  Living them all through all their memories?

There may be brains in yonder worlds of splendor
  Whose plentitude we might but so conceive
As we conceive those worlds themselves from slen-
    der
  Threads of the starlight they through darkness
    weave.

And, as they take our memories, they give us
  Thereby the resurrection; for, as heirs
Of all we were, they represent and live us,
  And are our very selves, as we are theirs.

V.

Thought so beyond that circle and the Medium,
  So outside all their doctrine's range and scope,
To them but jargon would have been and tedium,
  If he had spoken thus his faith and hope.

But he spoke not, save as he made denial
  Touching the dead; still pondering if part
The dead had had in that tranced woman's trial
  At reading secrets written in his heart.

Then was proposed to be experimented
  (The Lady's eyes grew smothered flame in smoke)
Whether, that night, conditions so consented
  That she might spirits into form invoke.

A side-room veiled off with a doorway's curtain,
  The spirit-rapturist there closeted,
The lights dimmed down to glimmering uncertain,
  And that hushed circle waiting for the dead!

Poor soul-sick longers for a fleshly witness
  Of immortality! O, dolorous!
With thirst, with hunger, yet with no more fitness
  To taste the everlasting life than thus!

But hist! The curtain rustled. and forth glided
  A woman, white-gowned, willowy of form,
With shower of hair, which her fair brow divided
  As doth the sun a parting summer-storm.

For but a moment that old awful shiver
  The heart takes from the presence of a wraith
Of child's credulity seemed to deliver
  Him over to the bonds of childhood's faith.

Near him she came; she seemed with love to linger;
  With raptured smile she stood beside him till,
As if forgetting, with unghostly finger
  She touched his forehead. Through him ran a
    thrill

From that warm touch, and up he sprang and
    caught her
  Fast in his arms. She strove not to arrest
His fervor; and, when full to light he brought her,
  He held the Medium weeping on his breast.

With speech too shallow for a thought to swim in,
  In faith whose fiction made a fool of fact,
That circle's long-haired men and short-haired
    women
  Huddled upon him and denounced his act.

His arms then from her gently disengaging,
  Bleeding afresh at love's old murder-scars,
He rushed, as from a mob of madmen raging,
  Out to the silent saneness of the stars.

O Stars! as the flakes of a snowstorm,
　How ye fly, and fall, and drift!
Swift snowing of suns out of darkness,
　Whirled by winds of Force and whiffed!
Fly! fall! but the wind the Almighty
　Still behind you always runs,
Still pushes you onward together,
　Fixed each sun in drift of suns.

Fixed, ay! to the vision of mortal
　Never change hath shown in you:
Seas, lands, and their kingdoms and races,
　All have changed, but ye are true;
Still true to the old constellations,
　Such as when man's forehead first
Up lifted itself to their glories
　With this human spirit's thirst.

Calm! still! though in every sparkle
　Motions like the thunderbolt,
Vast, vast as our measures of heaven—
　Planet's wheel and comet's volt—
All hang, as it were in a dewdrop
　Frozen to a steadfast gleam;
Place, time, braided in with the starlight,
　Whimseys of a far-off dream!

Drift! drift! all the universe drifting
 Round some orb too vast for thought!
On! on! awful maelstrom of matter! ,
 Wheeling in a gulf of naught!
Whirl! wheel! and my soul like a seabird
 Flies across, and dips and flees—
Wild wings of my soul, like the seabird's,
 Tost and lost upon the seas!

VI.

As if dropped suddenly back into body—
 For this had thither groped, apart from him—
He found his tired feet pressing those old soddy
 Paths of the churchyard in the twilight dim.

Life's madness now death's sadness fell: the mad-
 ness   ,
 That he had fled from, that had whirled and
  swung
The swift stars round his soul, fell to the sadness
 Of the green graves that there he lay among.

As thus he lay there looking up to starlight,
 Thus dreaming upward into heaven, appeared
To him a strange gleam, whether near or far light,
 Within him or without him, strange and weird.
 8

Into himself he gazed, and saw it looming
From far horizons, as a girdle drawn
About the whole sky, opening and blooming
From twilight into universal dawn.

It rose and grew, and presently a thrilling
Deliciousness of swiftness and a rush
Of radiance overcame his nature, stilling
His heartbeats into death's ecstatic hush.

SOME ECLOGS

SOME ECLOGS.

RAIN ON THE ROOF.

When the hovering humid darkness
  Over all the starry spheres
Flows and falls like sorrow softly
  Breaking into blessèd tears,
Then how sweet to press the pillow
  Of a cottage-chamber bed
And lie listening to the raindrops
  On the low roof overhead.

To the pitpat on the shingles
  Answer echoes in the heart;
And dim dreamy recollections
  Into form and being start,
And the busy fairy, Fancy,
  Weaves her air-threads, warp and woof,
As I listen to the patter
  Of the light rain on the roof.

Now in memory comes my mother
 As she used in summers gone,
Taking leave of little faces
 That her loving look shone on;
And I feel that fond look on me
 As I feel the old refrain
Here repeated on the shingles
 By the patter of the rain.

Then my little seraph-sister,
 With the wings and waving hair,
And her star-eyed cherub-brother—
 A serene angelic pair—
Glide around my wakeful pillow
 With sweet praise or mild reproof,
As I shut my eyes and listen
 To the soft rain on the roof.

And another comes, to thrill me
 With her eyes' bewitching blue,
And I mind not, musing on her,
 That my heart she never knew;
I remember but to love her
 With a passion kin to pain,
And my quickened pulses quiver
 To the patter of the rain.

Art hath naught of tone or cadence,
   Naught of music's magic spell,
That can thrill the secret fountain
   Whence the tears of rapture well,
Like that weird nocturne of Nature,
   That subdued, subduing strain
Which is played upon the shingles
   By the patter of the rain.

1849   1899.

SINGING FLAME.

A paean, Science! Thy cunning has found
(Cunning Science, a paean to thee!)
Singing Flame, where the forces agree
In all their marvelous protean round,
    Where light is to hear and sound is to see.

Song and the soul of the world are the same;
    Motion (the winged beginning of things)
    Is heat, by the sudden stop of its wings,
And heat is motion replumed with flame,
    And song is flame that quivers and sings.

As motion to heat, and heat to light,
    And light to flame of music is whirled,
    So the very flight of the stars is hurled
Into song from the secrets of night,
    And song keeps touch with the light of the world.

Ay, the soul of sound from the heart of fire
    Utters a flame, and the spirit hears
    Therein the light of a million years
Ago, sung down from the shining choir
    Of the morning-stars' jubilant spheres.

This is the light that old Wordsworth felt,
  Or dreamed with a vision keen and strong,
  Whose rays nor to land nor to sea belong,
But into a flame of melody melt—
Song that is flame and flame that is song.

This is the light that was pillar of smoke,
  Or only pillar of fire at most,
  To the marching, camping, carousing host,
But, when to the Red-Sea singer it spoke,
  Was a flaming tongue of the Holy Ghost.

This is the light that Dante pursued
  Through all the lurid regions of hell;
  That Milton saw in his blindness well;
That our miraculous Shakespeare indued
  With a glory no mortal can tell.

But the thin blue flame of these cultured years
  That shrinks and faints at the lilt of a breath,
  What is it this pale blue ardor saith
Of fears that are hopes, and hopes that are fears,
  And of deeps that are deeper than death?

Little it saith, and it singeth naught,
  But it creeps the ground along and about
  With delicate wreathings in and out,
And flickers away in a swoon of thought,
  And dies in a dainty dream of doubt.

And sometimes, too, it is hard to be told
  From lifted smoke, so it takes from Art
  Alone its aimless ethereal start;
For it has no flaming and singing hold
  . On the core of fire at Nature's heart.

O soul of that fire, O issue from night,
  And fuse all the twinklers, name by name,
  And melt to thy gold their azurine fame,
And pour down the heavens in wine of light,
  And fill all the world with Singing Flame!

VESUVIUS.

A PARABLE FOR THE WHITMANITES.

Old Vesuvius, calmly possessing its forces primeval,
Keeping them pent in its bosom as far, dim dreams
    of the passions
Which in its youth it had vented in red molten out-
    bursts of thunder,
Held its form and stood serene through ages and
    ages.
Men had forgotten its ravages. Villages clustered
    about it.
Peasantry climbed it with vineyards. The opulence,
    luxury, pleasure,
Learning of dissolute Italy lolled in the charm of
    its outskirts.
Spartacus banded his gladiatorial athletes for free-
    dom
Once in the top of it—safe in its great, broad cup,
    which was empty
Then, long then, of the wine of its wrath, where-
    withal it had staggered
When, through its mad young years in carouse with
    its comrades Titanic,

Ischia, Barbaro, Somma, Arsoni, and old Solfatara.

Mediterranean winds blew balm through its or-
chards and gardens.

West, and north, and east it swung, from sunrise to
sunset,

Slowly about its shoulders its long, wide mantle of
shadow,

Shielding the men at their toil on the slopes and the
birds at their singing.

Far to the folk coming in on the ships it appeared a
great pillar,

Steadfast prop of blue roof of sky over blue floor
of water,

While, aland, it showed itself bulked on the world's
gravitation,

Fixed of form and poised serene through ages and
ages.

Suddenly then, with a bellowing frenzy, it panted
out darkness

Over itself and the land and the sea; as a priest
gone apostate,

Tore off its miter and hurled it (renouncing the faith
with blaspheming)

Down on the worshipers; growing in rage, drew a
dagger of lightning,

Brandished, and slashed all its veins and bled hell-
fire. And the people,

Seeing sublimity gloom into horror, and day into
   midnight—
Majesty topple from cosmical forms into rubbishy
   ruin—
Rocks fly as meteors, chaos ejaculate flame, and
   with thunder
Sputter plutonian ashes and scoriac cinders—the
   people
Fled from the mountain, abandoning castle, and
   farmhouse, and villa,
Stumbling their perilous ways through the roar, and
   the stench, and the blackness
Out to the sun on the plain of Campania. Multi-
   tudes perished,
Whelmed by the fire-flakes that fell from the clouds
   of the smoke like a snowing.
Civilization forgot them for centuries. Stricken
   Pompeii,
Borne down under the deluge infernal, and smoth-
   ered and buried,
Sank out of memory, and no more was it known
   where its grave was.

Now, after hundreds and hundreds of years, is un-
   earthed the dead city.
Matter that once flew as flame in the heavens and
   startled an empire,

Dig it up, shovel it, cart it away, it is dirt and
   obstruction,
Hiding the relics of man and the rare forms of art
   he has fashioned.
Here in the marl is the mold of an old Roman sen-
   tinel's body,
Now more than eighteen centuries dead at the post
   of his duty.
Here is the exquisite ring of a bride whose love is
   immortal.
Here is the beautiful dwelling of Sallust. Here the-
   ater, forum,
Where Rome's language, whose ghost, from the
   Church, still haunteth the nations,
Lived on the stage and the rostrum—in greeting of
   neighbor to neighbor—
Shouted the plays of the school-children here in the
   streets. And the temples,
Here they stand in the full broad day of the worship
   of Jesus,
Shockingly waked from their obsolete gods as from
   dreams in a nightmare.

What the spontaneous gush from yon old and familiar volcano,
Violent, formless, beside these reminders of man and
   his labors?
Yet the volcano had covered all these and preserved
   them for ages.

THE SEA-POWER.

American, English, Old-Teuton are we;
  Kindred race, the same speech, and like law make
    us one,
And old wars with each other have made us both
    free:
So, for freedom as one let our two banners be
  Wheresoever the tides of the high seas run,
  Flag with flag, ship with ship, and great gun with
    great gun.

Let the old Union-Jack with Old Glory ally,
  Asking not of the past which was right or which
    wrong,
And the two on the sea may together defy
All the flags all the rest of the Powers can fly,
  And command the peace to their lands for as long
  As the Eagle is swift and the Lion is strong.

To ally for the help and not for the harm
  Of the peace of all lands and their freedom and
    right,
To dispel one another's distrust and alarm,

To impel one another in trust to disarm,
　And to rid their taxed toil of war's burden and
　　blight—
　Only that be the Sea-Power's mission of might.

As the Sea-Power goes with the sea round the
　　world,
　With the sea round the lands and between land
　　and land,
To the lands from the sea (where its flags are un-
　　furled)
Its mandates shall come as the billows are hurled
　On the beach or in ripples received on the sand—
　As the right to persuade or the might to com-
　　mand.

Such the Anglo-American Sea-Power be!
　Let its flags on the sea fly together as one—
Though as two on the land, always one on the sea—
Ay, America, England, Japan, may the three
　Flock together wherever the high seas run,
　Flag with flag, ship with ship, and great gun with
　　great gun.

1898.

THE WOODBIRD.

Oh! wildwood, wildwood, wildwood!
It is a weird note so repeated;
  Lyric startled from its theme;
A song by some faint shock defeated,
Or perchance the uncompleted
  Sad forgetting of a dream.

Give sunlight for the lark and robin,
  Sun, and sky, and mead, and bloom;
But give, for this rare throat to throb in
And this lonesome soul to sob in,
  Wildwoods, with their green and gloom.

Oh! wildwood, wildwood, wildwood!
In dim ravines he flits and perches,
  And he listens in the glen,
And, like a palmer in old churches,
All the solemn shrines he searches
  For remission and amen.

9

Within great trees he sits and ponders
  Melodies his heart receives,
Till all in that one trill he squanders—
Echo of the dream that wanders
  Through the silent sleep of leaves.

Oh! wildwood, wildwood, wildwood!
That strain of his is his despairing
  Of how little can be told ;
Yet that is more than all the daring,
·Loud, familiar throats' declaring
  With their bugle-notes of gold.

All these the mockbird catches featly ;
  Keen roulade and warbled whim
He strings upon his carol sweetly,
But my woodbird's cry completely
  Flieth and eludeth him.

For this is voicing of such places
  As the mimic never sees ;
A rune of old Druidic traces,
Chant from old cathedral spaces
  In a thousand years of trees.

Oh! wildwood, wildwood, wildwood!
Were he to you his music bringing,
    You might fault his monotone;
But not to you his little singing
Soul of fire its flame is flinging—
    Sings he for himself alone.

OUR ONLY DAY.

Were this our only day,
  Did not our yesterdays and morrows give
To hope and memory their interplay,
  How should we bear to live?

Not merely what we are,
  But what we were and what we are to be,
Makes up our life—the far days each a star,
  The near days nebulae.

At once would love forget
  Its keen pursuits and coy delays of bliss,
And its delicious pangs of fond regret,
  Were there no day but this.

And who, to win a friend,
  Would to the secrets of his heart invite
A fellowship that should begin and end
  Between a night and night?

Who, too, would pause to prate
  Of insult or remember slight or scorn,
Who would this night lie down to sleep with hate,
  Were there to be no morn?

Who would take heed to wrong,
  To misery's complaint or pity's call,
The long wail of the weak against the strong,
  If this one day were all?

And what were wealth with shame,
  The vanity of office, pride of caste,
The winy sparkle of the bubble fame,
  If this day were the last?

Ay, what were all days worth,
  Were there no looking backward or before;
If every human life that drops to earth
  Were lost forevermore?

But each day is a link
  Of days that pass and never pass away:
For memory and hope—to live, to think—
  Each is our only day.

OHIO CENTENNIAL ODE.

Delivered in the Coliseum, Columbus, O., on the Opening
Day, September 4th, 1888, of the State cele-
bration of the Centennial Year.

In what historic thousand years of man
  Has there been builded such a State as this?
Yet, since the clamor of the axes ran
  Along the great woods, with the groan and hiss
And crash of trees, to hew thy groundsels here,
  Ohio, but a century has gone,
And thy republic's building stands the peer
  Of any that the sun and stars shine on.
Not on a fallen empire's rubbish-heap,
  Not on old quicksands wet with blood of wrong,
Do the foundations of thy structure sleep,
  But on a ground of nature, new and strong.
Men that had faced the Old World seven years
  In battle on the Old World turned their backs
And, quitting Old-World thoughts and hopes and
    fears,
  With only rifle, powder-horn, and axe

For tools of civilization, won their way
  Into the wilderness, against wild man and beast,
And laid the wood-glooms open to the day,
  And from the sway of savagery released
The land to nobler uses of a higher race;
  Where Labor, Knowledge, Freedom, Peace, and
    Law
Have wrought all miracles of dream in place
  And time—ay, more than ever dream foresaw.

A hundred years of Labor! Labor free!
  Our River ran between it and the Curse,
And freemen proved how toil can glory be.
  The heroes that Ohio took to nurse
    (As the she-wolf the founders of old Rome)—
Their deeds of fame let history rehearse
And oratory celebrate; but see
    This paradise their hands have made our home!
Nod, plumes of wheat, wave, banderoles of corn,
  Toss, orchard-oriflammes, swing, wreaths of vine,
  Shout, happy farms, with voice of sheep and kine,
    For the old victories conquered here on these
The fields of Labor when, ere we were born,
    The fathers fought the armies of the trees,
  And; chopping out the night, chopt in the morn!

A hundred years of Knowledge! We have mixt
  More brains with Labor in the century
Than man had done since the decree was fixt
  That labor was his doom and dignity.
All honor to those far-foreworking men
  Who, as they stooped their sickles in to fling,
  Or took the wheat upon their cradles' swing,
Thought of the boy, the little citizen
There gathering sheaves, and planned the school for
    him,
  Which should wind up the clockwork of his mind
To cunning moves of wheels and blades that skim
  Across the fields, and reap, and rake, and bind!
They planned the schools—the woods were full of
    schools!
Our learning has not soared, but it has spread:
Ohio's intellects are sharpened tools
  To deal with daily fact and daily bread.
The starry peaks of knowledge in thin air
  Her culture has not climbed, but on the plain,
In whatsoever is to do or dare
  With mind or matter, there behold her reign.
The axemen who chopt out the clearing here
  Where stands the Capital, could they today
  Arise and see our hundred years' display—
Steam-wagons in their thundering career—

Wires that a friend's voice waft across a State,
And wires wherein imprisoned lightnings wait
    To leap forth at the turning of a key—
Could they these shows of mind in matter note,
    Machines that almost conscious souls confess,
    Seeming to will and think—the printing-press,
Not quite intelligent enough to vote—
Could they arise these marvels to behold,
    What would to them the past Republic seem—
The State historified in volumes old,
    Or prophesied in Grecian Plato's dream?

A hundred years of Freedom! Freedom such
    No other people on the earth had known
    Till our America the world had shown
What Freedom meant. No foot of slave might
        touch
Our earth, no master's lash outrage our heaven:
    The Declaration of the Great July,
Fired by our Ordinance of Eightyseven,
    Flamed from the River to the northern sky;—
Ay, that flame rose against the arctic stars,
    And shone a new aurore across the land.
A Body scored with stripes of whip and scars
    Of branding-iron seemed to understand—

Soulless though reckoned by our Union's pact—
That It was Man, for whom that heavenly sign
Lit up the North; and while the bloodhounds
    tracked
Him footsore through Kentucky, stars benign
Befriended him and brought him to our shore,
    A stranger, frightened, hungry, travel-worn;
And we laid hands on him and gave him o'er
    Again to bondage, as in fealty sworn.
So rich in freedom, we had none to give!
    While we might quaff, we could not pass the cup:
No slave should touch foot on our soil and live
    Upon it slave—he must be given up!
When that first man was wrested from our State,
    Then slavery had crossed the Rubicon;
Then Freedom was the whole Republic's fate;
    Then John Brown's soul began its marching-on;
Then the 'Ohio Idea' had to go
    Where'er the banner of the Union flew,
From northmost limits in Alaskan snow
    To southmost in the Mexic waters blue.

A hundred years of Peace! Yes, less the four
    (Our little Indian squabbles were not war),
The four when we, in battle's shock and roar,
    Declared that Freedom was worth dying for.

Ohio gave to that great fight for Man
Her Grant, her Sherman, and her Sheridan,
And her victorious hundred thousands more.
Victorious, yes, though legions of them sleep
 In garments rolled in blood on foughten fields—
Though still the mothers and the widows weep
 For the slain heroes borne home on their shields.
Their glorious victory this day behold:
 They conquered Peace; and where their manly
  frays
Across the land of bondage stormed and rolled,
 Millions of grateful freedmen hymn their praise.
Ohio honors them with happy tears:
 The battles that they braved for her,
 The banner that they waved for her,
 The freedom that they saved for her,
Shall keep their laurels green a thousand years.

A hundred years of Law! The people's will,
 The might of the majority,
 The right of the minority,
 The light hand with authority
We promised, with the purpose to fulfill.
But the contagion of the border-taint
 Blackened our statutes with its shameful stain,

And left the color of our conscience faint
Till freshened by the battle-storm's red rain.
Ay, war has legislated; it has cast
The 'White Man's Government' out into night,
And Labor, Knowledge, Freedom, Peace, at last
Stand color-blind in Law's resplendent light.

Now hail, my State of States! thy justice wins—
Thy justice and thy valor now are one;
Thou hast arisen, and thy little sins
Are spots of darkness lost upon the sun.
Thy sun is up—O, may it never set!—
These hundred years were but thy morning-red:
It shall be forenoon for thy glory yet
When all who this day look on thee are dead.
O, splendor of the noon awaiting thee!
O, rights of man and hights of manhood free!
Hail, beautiful Ohio that shalt be!
Hail! Ship of State! and take our parting cheers!
Ah, God! that we might gather here to see
Thy sails loom in swoln with a thousand years!

THE LAST MEETING.

I met you last night on a lone country road ;
  The fields either side were green with the May,
  The birds were full song (you had made the night
    day),
And a sapphire sky with a golden sun glowed.

And you hurried to me in your fine old way—
  Imperious passion aflame I could see
  In your eyes as of old, when in love were we—
And you seized my arm and commanded me,
    "Stay !"

And you questioned, "What is it you ask of me?"
  You clung to me close as we walked, and each
    side
  The birds from the thickets and treetops replied,
Singing, "Love! the old love! only love asks he!"

Then your brow grew stern and you bitterly cried,
  "There is darkness between us!"—and sleep
    closed in :
  I awoke in the dark where the dream had been,
And watched all alone till the sad night died.

CHILD LOST.

She came the sweet fulfillment of a dream;
  She bloomed upon me like a flower;
  Her life was my life's gift and dower,
Her love was my love's meed supreme.

She seemed a precious memory of mine
  Waked from the holiness of death
  And quickened back to pulse and breath
By working of love's miracle divine.

I took her babehood as a gift of God;
  And when her tiny toddling feet
  Began my coming-home to meet,
My heart lay under every step she trod.

Her life was light to me where night had been;
  It was herself she heralded
  When from her little crib she said
Each morning, "Papa, light is coming in."

She was a newness and a solace deep—
  A newness like the dawning light,
  A solace like the lulling night,
A joy like waking, and a bliss like sleep.

Her being was around me as a sky
  Of summer is around the earth:
  I never thought of any worth
Of life without her love to price it by.

But suddenly I missed the child one day;
  I looked, and lo a stranger stood
  There stately in full womanhood
Where I had left the little maid at play.

MARS—AUGUST 1892.

Thou splendid sparkle of the sun,
Noon-lighted hemisphere of golden Mars,
Now once again thou from the farther stars
Thy hithermost career hast run.

Thou blazest to our Aryan eyes
Not as on Hindoo-Koosh or on the slope
Of old Armenia, ere the telescope
Fetched down to us the upper skies.

Nor art thou more a flaming targe,
As for old Latin Mavors, god of war,
Or for the old Norse god of thunder, Thor,
To dazzle in the battle-charge.

For science now sees thee a world,
And fancy peoples thee with brother-men,
As thou and Earth approach and greet again,
Nearest the solar center whirled.

O ship of heaven, as we go by,
Might we across the deep some signal show
To let the voyagers upon thee know
    That not alone they sail the sky!

But what they are to us we are
To them, a glory-mystery of the night—
The rising and the setting of a light,
    Their morning and their evening star.

Dead silence, and all-killing cold,
And twoscore million miles of twixt-abyss
Shall still the race of that world and of this
    Forever from each other hold.

Although that sunlit globe may swarm
With myriads of living, on its face
Our glasses glimpse, from this terrestrial place,
    Not even a mote of living form.

Who holds his head among the stars
With pride of fame or fortune here on Earth
May well take estimation of 'his worth
    By looking at himself from Mars.
    10

THE SHADOW.

When first I saw my soul it was the sun
    Just risen from the underworld of light;
I did not see the Shadow which had then begun
    To go with me a heritage of night.

My face was toward the morn, the birds in song
    Set me to music, while that Shadow's black
Sketch of my small new self lay large along
    The level of the future at my back.

All forenoon still I faced my mounting soul,
    My southward sun, and scarcely was aware
Of this dark wraith which northward round me stole
    And seemed to creep to me from out the air.

At noon I turned, and close before my feet
    The shortened Shadow faint and feeble lay:
So much my life's meridian light and heat
    Had wrought the power of darkness into day.

With ardor now I seek the sun once more,
    As down the slope of afternoon it wheels;
But, though my feet seem flame-winged as before,
    I feel the Shadow dogging at my heels.

I feel the Shadow, and I find my face
  Turn toward it and my back turn toward the
    light;
I see the Shadow lengthen to retrace
  My path across the day from night to night.

OLD GLORY.

Written for the Military Order of the Loyal Legion of the
United States, and Dedicated to the Com-
mandery of Ohio, May 6, 1891.

When hope unfurled thee rainbow-barred,
Red, white, and blue, and thirteen-starred,
    Gloria! Old Gloria!
The Fathers pledged their lives to guard
Thy sacred folds, though battle-scarred,
And hand thy glory down unmarred,
    Gloria! Old Gloria!

Flag of the Declaration when
The sword was whetted with the pen,
    Gloria! Old Gloria!
Flag of the Constitution then!
To hold the old stars three and ten,
And double them again, again,
    Gloria! Old Gloria!

But when from thee some went to fall
The legions moved at Lincoln's call,
    Gloria! Old Gloria!

With bayonets round thee a wall,
They struck the chains from every thrall,
And fixed the stars for good and all,
    Gloria! Old Gloria!

By that supreme American
Slain in the hour of mercy's plan,
    Gloria! Old Gloria!
By Grant, and Sherman, Sheridan,
And all the dead, both chief and man,
We wave thee still in freedom's van,
    Gloria! Old Gloria!

By all our living heroes, too,
Who stood to thee in battle true,
    Gloria! Old Gloria!
Who pined for thee the prisons through,
And suffered more than death could do—
We hoist Old Glory high for you!
    Gloria! Old Gloria!

And when all these, as soon they must,
March on, march on to join the just,
    Gloria! Old Gloria!

When their old guns and swords are rust,
Heaven hold thee still our country's trust,
And kiss thee proud above their dust,
    Gloria! Old Gloria!

Thee as an angel's pinion fair
We will for peace with honor bear,
    Gloria! Old Gloria!
But if a foe thy war shall dare,
Make him in sorrow thee declare
Prince of the powers of the air,
    Gloria! Old Gloria!

Flag of the Union, float and fly
O'er land and sea in all the sky,
    Gloria! Old Gloria!
And as thy State-stars multiply,
Group them together all so nigh
That they shall blaze one sun on high,
    Old Glory! Glory! Gloria!

CYGNI CARMEN MORITURI.

Ocean! I feel it—I hear in my spirit
  Echoing pulse of its billows that thunder
In on the beaches, and now, as I near it,
  Hope in me rises, and longing, and wonder.

What it is like I have dreamed, but I know not—
  Vastness, and silence, and freedom, and motion,
Tides that flow on, and abysses that flow not—
  All I shall see, I shall be of the ocean!

Stream that hast wafted me, widening River,
  Hither from inland afar where thy source is,
Far thou hast wafted me, here to deliver
  Me to the sea, where the end of thy course is.

Me and my memories—fountain-brook plashings,
  Pauses in pools through the cool woods, and sal-
    lies
Thence along rapids, down waterfalls' dashings,
  Out to the gliding of creeks in the valleys;

Flocking with kindred in blue lakes, and nesting
  Oft on the summer-green shores, but returning
Ever to follow the flow never-resting
  (Life's with thy current's flow oceanward yearn-
    ing)—

Me and my memories, sicknesses, sorrows,
  Old age's loneliness, all thou art bringing
Down to the deep and the night—but tomorrow's
  Joy of the sea in my spirit is singing!

SEA-SONNETS TOWARD ITALY.

To My Daughters on the Atlantic.

I.

You seem to go across the gulf of death
  Which parts the two worlds; for it is as though
  You had died yesterday and here below
We were expecting when your spirit-breath
  Should pulse back through the dark to make us
    know
That you were traversing the deep no more,
  No more were passing from this world of ours,
But had arrived safe on the happy shore.
  Could I feel forward to that land of flowers,
Dream over to that Florence waiting you,
  Sleep over seas and nights and days between,
To wake in Italy and greet you two,
  I would forego the life to intervene,
  So to forefeel and dream and sleep serene.

Xenia, 2 October, 1890.

II.

Today I saw the sun rise, and it brought
   Back to my memory, poppied yet with sleep,
   The sudden thought of you upon the deep;
The great sun rose from you a sudden thought
   To fill the world again. I seemed to leap
Its level rays and ride them to your sky
   Of forenoon: from its orb I looked down thence
And spied your ship thereunder going by.
   I would have given you intelligence
From home, could I have conjured on that orb
   A spot shaped throbbing from this heart of mine
And on your hearts a magic to absorb
   The meaning of it. But the dazzling shine
   Was all you saw of my sun-dream divine.

Xenia, 4 October, 1890.

III.

Did I not realize, as you do now
   By your straight speed east on it these four days,
   How vast the world is, I should dread the haze
Which glooms this morning; but your vessel's prow
   May point to clear sun, and its forenoon-blaze

May pour your sea-floored sky-tent full of gold:
  So there for you were youth and Orient,
While west the sad sky mists, and I am old.
  I dream it so; but dreams do not content;
For in my thought, clouds darken, great winds rise,
  And billows toss you, and I long to stand
Beside you there, and hold you in my eyes,
  And cling to you with father's heart and hand,
  Dear mariners a thousand miles from land!

Xenia, 5 October, 1890.

IV.

No stars here last night, and another day
  Has risen westering from you to stain
  The blue with scud of clouds betokening rain;
Contrary breezes whiffle, and I pray
  They east not into gales to dance the main
Of the Atlantic—But, lo now amid
  This line, they blow away the curtaining dark
In tatters, and let sunlight that was hid
  Peep through by snatches; and again your bark
Catches joy-sparkles from my swells of hope,
  Which heave and help you shoreward; and I
    dream

You fleeting down the round world's water-slope
  Safe into haven: soon a lightning-gleam
  With greets from you shall through the ocean
    stream!

Xenia, 6 October, 1890.

OLD VIRGINIA.

O Virginia! Mother of Liberty!
  What memories surround thee!
  What glories have crowned thee!
What honor and praise
When thy great Burgess Henry stood
And spoke, for all the sisterhood
  Of the old colonial days,
Words that were not merely breath,
Words that thy grand history saith—
'Give me liberty or give me death!'
The Revolution round thee formed;
  Thou took its battles on thy breast,
  And on thy plumed defiant crest
The fiercest British thunder stormed.
Thou wast in when the fight began
For our America's freedom of man;
  And through it all there stood thy sons
  With thy sisters' bravest, foremost ones;
Ay, to thee at home and in the van
  The foe surrendered his guns.
The great Republic of the Free
Can never lose its pride in thee
  And thy past, Old Virginia!

O Virginia, Mother of Washington!
How blest among mothers!
More blest than all others
Of story and song
When heaven on thy bosom smiled
And thou brought forth the chief man-child
Of these many centuries long.
Thine his wise and manly youth,
Thine his chivalry and truth,
Thine his fame, intact of Envy's tooth,
And proof against the tooth of Time.
Such manhood's majesty and weight
Made Old Dominion of thy State,
And made thy leadership sublime.
Thou didst great, but thy greatest deed,
When our America's uttermost need
Demanded greatest deeds be done,
Was thy gift to her of Washington;
For the Nation under his strong lead
Became the Many in One;
The life, deeds, words, that Union meant,
The Union's Captain, President,
Were thy gift, Old Virginia!

O Virginia, Mother of Jefferson!
  The grand Declaration
  Which gave to the Nation
Its birth among men,
Thou hast the glory, too, of that
In thy illustrious Democrat
  Who was Old Virginia's pen
Rights of manhood to express—
Rights of all men to possess
Life, and liberty, and happiness.
A strong young eagle's voice it went
  Out on the glad winds to impeach
  The ancient tyrannies and preach
The gospel of new government.
That Great Writ was the one more act
For our American liberties' pact
  Which gives us claim on thee to call
  For monition to the Union all
That from Jefferson our faith and fact
  Of freedom never shall fall;
Thy breast's old loyal battle-rents,
Thy motherhood of Presidents,
  Speak for thee, Old Virginia!

THE END OF THE RAINBOW.

There is a rare region
    Whose heavenward scope
Holds legion on legion
    Of angels of hope—
        At the end of the rainbow.

Endure the dull present,
    Its toil, moil, and sorrow!
We shall all find that pleasant
    Elysium tomorrow—
        At the end of the rainbow.

There the sky never varies
    From glory to gloom ;
There groves and green prairies
    Eternally bloom—
        At the end of the rainbow.

The bees hive no honey
    In that happy land ;
For the days are all sunny,
    The air always bland—
        At the end of the rainbow.

There Hope climbs the mountains
  And rests in the sky;
There Peace drinks at fountains
  That never go dry—
    At the end of the rainbow.

There joys above measure
  Are blisses benign;
There life's ruby, pleasure,
  Melts into sweet wine—
    At the end of the rainbow.

There Love from its madness
  Of longing and moan
Leaps whole in the gladness
  Of finding its own—
    At the end of the rainbow.

No shadow Cimmerian
  Of ignorance there;
But full the Pierian
  Spring jets in the air—
    At the end of the rainbow.

There glitter the riches
That time never rusts;
There glory's proud niches
  Are filled with our busts—
    At the end of the rainbow.

Endure the dull present,
  Its toil, moil, and sorrow;
We shall all find the pleasant
  Elysium tomorrow—
    At the end of the rainbow.

IS LIFE WORTH LIVING?

You ask, in scorn, if life is worth the living.
  But tell me, then, what is it you call life?
Is it the joy of getting or of giving?
  Is it repose of thought or thrill of strife?

Who toils from rising of the sun to setting,
  And robs his nights of peace, and murders sleep,
Giving his whole soul to the greed of getting,
  Gets no possession that the soul can keep.

The young rich man who turned away in sadness
  When Jesus bade him all his riches give
Had never tasted how the heavenly gladness
  Of making others glad helps one to live.

His life is not worth living who remembers
  No other living than of self and sense;
To kindle warmth and light in such dead embers
  Were past the power of Omnipotence.

Nor deem that in pursuit of pure thought solely
  (The palefaced passions back of prison-bars)
You ever reach the hight of living wholly;
  Go forth in night and think among the stars!

If majesties of worlds there do not crush you,
    Nor miracles of distance hold you fast,
Nor mysteries of motion awe and hush you,
    You are not living then in thought, at last.

Yet if you were, the keen eternal yearning
    To know what never can be known would make
A mockery of all your little learning—
    The thirst that no Pierian spring can slake.

But, since high thinking is not life's fruition,
    Try action—Is not that the life indeed?
To struggle for the prizes of ambition?
    To rule in council or in battle lead?

Ah, vanity! on wings of fancy rising,
    Behold earth through a million miles of air—
Man and the monuments of his devising
    All blank and silent in her moony glare.

But then?   There is, above the life's illusions,
    Above its greed and strife and pride, above
Death and the grave and faith's and doubt's confu-
        sions,
    One life worth living—love, love's joy of love.

•

THE HAUNTING VOICE.

The voice of a woman forever
  Runs sobbing after my soul;
Night or day, day or night, I can never
  Escape its mournful control;
  Its moaning musical dole
Pursues me for ever and ever.

It comes to my memory mingling
  With words it uttered of yore,
When its tones through my pulses went tingling
  With thrills felt never before—
  With thrills felt now nevermore,
Not even in home's holy mingling.

Says the sorrowful voice, "O my darling,
  Did love that being endow
Whose prattle outcarols the starling
  And makes home happier now?
  You took the marital vow,
And you gave me to die, O my darling!"

So forever this voice of a woman
  Cries desolately to me—
This voice as really human
  As voice of human can be!
  No matter whither I flee,
Still I hear this voice of a woman.

Down to death and the sepulcher's portal
  This voice shall follow my sin—
O, what if the voice is immortal,
  And, where hope's blisses begin,
  Shall come and welcome me in
With joy through the heavenly portal!

CONSUMMATION.

Death had sunk the world from under my feet;
  Love had given thee wings to fly;
And we met as the dawn and the darkness meet—
  Thou the dawn, and the darkness I.

My soul was a gloom that had blotted heaven;
  And thine was a fine ascending fire
That streamed it through with a luminous leaven
  Of hope of morning and day's desire.

Love wrought the miracle of raising the dead;
  Though on the tomb the seal had been put,
Thine eyes to my buried passion said,
  'Come forth!' and it came, bound hand and foot.

Sad memory drowned itself in those eyes—
  Fell into their liquid deeps and sunk;
And the darkness of all the earth and skies
  To those two crystals of darkness shrunk.

When we met our fate—rememberst the place?
My day was barren, my dream was done;
But the bright warm flush of thy radiant face
On my frozen heart flamed like a sun.

That look! it created the world anew:
Thy presence came to me like the sweep
Of a full white sail to the sudden view
Of a shipwrecked man on the deep.

I knew I was saved; I knew that thy voice
Should sing the cries in the night to peace;
But I felt it almost a guilt to rejoice
That love from the dead had love's release.

Thou hadst never suffered, and couldst not know
How past and present in me were whirled—
How the breeze out of sunrise seemed to blow
From the sundown of the underworld.

But Love is a god, and to him one day
Is a thousand years that are past:
I woke from the dreams that had flown away,
And, behold, they were true at last.

It seemed we had dwelt in the Morningstar
  Ere the soul of either was born;
And I saw thy face in glimmerings far
  Of memory's earliest morn.

The barefooted little damsel that played
  With me in the plash on the marge
Of the blue Ke-u-ka was flashed and rayed
  In the beam of this love so large.

Thy passionate voice, so sweetly that robbed
  My soul of its will and made it slave,
Was the girl Fanny Wolcott's when she sobbed
  My heart from me at her father's grave.

The victorious eyes that once I had met
  And mistaken for heavenly blue
Were dark as that night I remember yet,
  Because they were thine and were true.

Thou seemed the soul after death from the eve
  When we strolled Miami's green shore
And heard the cricket and katydid grieve
  That with them we should tryst no more.

The two strong loves that had fought for my heart
  And at last laid them down and smiled
To divide and rend it to graves apart
  Arose in thee and were reconciled.

From kiss on the sweet sad face in the night,
  From tears for the night-wind's human moan,
O! the waking to find, in love's new light,
  All faces, all voices thy own!

ESSAYS IN LITERAL TRANSLATION OF HOMERIC METERS.

ILIAD I. 1-32.

Sing, O goddess, the wrath of the Peleidéan
    Achilles,
Deadly, that brought innumerable sorrows upon
    the Achaians,
Sending untimely the mighty souls many of heroes
    to Hades,
And of the heroes themselves making ravin for dogs
    and for birds feast—
Yet, too, the counsel of Zeus was fulfilling—from
    when first in quarrel
Parted Atreides, chief of the warriors, and godlike
    Achilles.

Which of the gods was it set them contending
    together in quarrel?
It was the son of Leto and Zeus; for, against the
    chief angered,
All through the camp he inflicted a plague, and the
    soldiers were dying,

Since unto Chryses (the priest) had Atreides done a
  dishonor.
For he had come to the Achaians' fleet ships to de-
  liver his daughter,
He, that priest, and had brought gifts of ransom un-
  told, with a fillet
Held in his hands on a truncheon of gold, as the
  badge of Apollo,
Far-shooting archer, and suppliant pleaded with all
  the Achaians,
But above all with the two sons of Atreus, the
  army's commanders:
  "O Atreides twain and ye others, ye well-
    greaved Achaians,
Pray I indeed that the gods, who have their abode
  on Olympus,
Give you to plunder the city of Priam and well to
  fare homeward,
Only I pray you release my dear child and accept
  these her ransom,
Holding in reverence Zeus's son, far-shooting
  archer Apollo."

  Then all the other Achaians assentingly
    shouted in favor
Both of revering the priest and of taking the bounti-
  ful ransom.

This, though, pleased not the mind of the Atreus-
son Agamemnon,
But with abuse he sent him away and in stern
speech charged him:

"Let not me, old man, in the midst of the hol-
low ships find thee,
Either delaying now or back again coming hereafter,
Lest thee haply the deity's mace and fillet defend
not.
But this girl I will not release; ay, rather shall old
age
Come upon her, afar from her country, in our home
at Argos,
Plying to and fro at the loom and my bed for me
serving.
But go; do not provoke me, that safe thou be in
departing."

ILIAD III. 421-436.

So, when they reached Alexandros's passingly-
beautiful mansion,
Forthwith then did the handmaids turn to their
tasks, but the lady,

She the divine one of women, went into the high-
vaulted chamber.

And, then getting a chair for her, smile-loving
Aphrodite

Brought it, the goddess, and set it down so as to
face Alexandros.

There Helen took her seat, aegis-bearing Zeus's
daughter,

Backward turning her eyes, and tauntingly spoke to
her husband:

"So, thou hast come from the battle; thou
oughtest thy life to have lost there,

Slain at the hands of the warrior strong who once
was my husband.

Ere now, surely, thy boast was that thou didst ex-
cel Menelaos

Favored-of-Ares, both with thy strength, and hands,
and war-spear;

Nay, but go now and give Menelaos the favored-of-
Ares

Challenge again to confront thee in battle—But no,
I, even I urge

Thee to refrain and not in close combat with blond
Menelaos

Recklessly fight, lest quickly by him with the spear
thou be vanquished."

ILIAD VIII. 542-565.

Hector thus harangued, and loudly the Trojans
applauded.
Then they the sweating steeds loosed from the
yoke, and with halters they fastened
Each beside his car his own; and they had from the
city
Oxen and great sheep speedily driven and heart-
honey wine got,
Bread, too, out of their homes, and large store of
firewood they gathered.
Then to the gods immortal they sacrificed heca-
tombs perfect,
Whose steam-savor the winds bore out of the plain
into heaven.
And, high-hearted, upon the between-line ridges of
battle
All night long they sat, and their watchfires many
were burning.
And, as when in the heavens the stars shine forth
resplendent
Round the bright moon, when the air on high is
without any wind's breath;
Plain all the mountain-peaks show, and the fore-
lands' ends, and the valleys;

And from the heavens the infinite deep of the air
    overhead breaks,
Where are seen all the stars, and the shepherd at
    heart is delighted ;
So in the midst from the ships to the streams of the
    Xanthos the watchfires
Manifold lit by the Trojans appeared before Ilios
    blazing.
Ay, by the thousand the watchfires blazed in the
    plain, and beside them,
Fifty beside each fire, the men sat in the glare of
    the flame-light.
There too the steeds stood champing the white bar-
    ley-grain and the spelt-seed
Fast by their chariots, waiting the Dawn-goddess
    thronèd in glory.

MY LORD.

Ennobled? O Lord Alfred Tennyson!—
Now dare the curse, dig Shakespeare's bones
From underneath the Stratford-stones
And with a lordship prank the skeleton!

Men well may jeer and ask how thou has gained
  The right to have thy race renewed
  And thy old Saxon red blood blued
By royal warrant, clarified, and strained.

What hast thou done that goes to make a lord?
  The greatness by estate-in-tail
  Which Nature gives the first-born male
Thou canst not claim as Art's reward.

Is not true greatness, like the poet, born?
  Nobility of pedigree
  May well by birthright look on thee
With half a dozen centuries of scorn.

Where are thy old manorial parks and halls,
  A king's gift to a courtier's smile,
  Or loot of French braves when the Isle
Was theirs and Englishmen were churls and thralls?
12

Where is the half-mile's length of corridor
    Lined each side with thy pictured row
    Of ancestors, whose grand airs show
The highness born above the need to soar?

With none of these beginnings, dost thou dare
    To ape the greatness of the great?
    Can Genius ancestors create—
Make old halls of its castles-in-the-air?

Genius may work its miracles with time—
    May make past present and forelive
    The future; but it cannot give
Blood-heirship of antiquity sublime.

But shall Caste's colorless anachronism
    Change to the rainbow's living hues
    And glory to thy sons diffuse
By being passed through thy poetic prism?

Pity the son with intellect too numb
    To see that thy one natal word
    Surnames him over all absurd
Tinsel of titles known to Christendom!

A BIRD'S AUTUMN LYRIC.

Out of south flew up together
    She and I;
Moods of love like April weather
    Made our sky;
May in egg and June in feather,
    Such of fashion
    Grew our passion,
  Till the summer filled with singing
  And with heavenly-blissful winging,
And our oneness dreamed not whether
    I were she or she were I.

Robed she russet to my golden,
    And for song
She to me was all beholden;
    Mornings long
She would muse me in the olden
    Treetop's twilight,
    And I fly, light,
  Spring and flash, 'dart back and flitter,
  Coo and call, till her sweet twitter
Would my ecstasy embolden
    To a burst and rush of song.

But of new love with her breast full
    Then she yearned
Melancholy and unrestful;
    And she spurned,
Though I sang the east and west full,
    All my duty,
    All my beauty—
Of my plumage all the flower,
Of my piping all the power:
Toward the lately brooded nestful
    All her being backward turned.

Now we mope through autumn waning,
    She and I,
Nor in shining nor in raining
    Trill or cry
Each to other ever deigning
    Of the olden
    Passion golden
With the south and April weather;
Yet we mate and wait together
Till, from pining and from plaining,
    Vanish sunward she and I.

THE SHIBBOLETH.

Written by invitation of the Western Association of
Writers for reading in their Convention at
Warsaw, Indiana, July 10, 1889.

The gods are all dead—glory be to God!
Though still they ghost it in old words, as Pan,
Apollo, Jove, the Numen (or the Nod),
That cast thin shadows in the thought of man,
Yet they themselves have toppled from their hight
Olympian and fallen back to clod.
Science has exorcised them with its light;
Religion banished them from fane and shrine:
Only in Poesy they haunt the night,
Pale reminiscences of life divine.

Now that the Christ has come, inonoclast
Of old religions, now that Science flings
Its dawn-flame on the darkness of the past,
And fetches into sun the truth of things,
Why is it that Imagination moons?
Why is it Poesy still sits and sings
The babe-songs of old fairyland and croons
Her mother-melodies of ignorance,

Her Indian mimicries of Finnish runes,
  Her Holy Grails, her Arthurs of romance?

Why with Endymion still fondly mope,
  Shaping Love's Lady out of moonshine—why,
Unless our Poesy is past all hope
  And pining with the Muses Nine to die?
The Nine are every one already dead;
  It is their airy ghosts that linger nigh;
They all, with god Apollo at their head,
  · They all would not be air enough to blow
The sail of Chambered Nautilus aspread
  And push it over Prose's undertow.

It seems not strange that our new world of Fact
  Should look on Verse as an anachronism—
A stopping of the white light to refract
  Its rays to colors through old Fancy's prism—
Nay, juggling with the light, in darkened rooms,
  By Fancy's worn-out tricks of spiritism.
While lived the gods the words of Song were
      blooms
  Upon the tree of life; but such words now
Are withered garlands on the dead gods' tombs,
  Dry wreaths around a marble Muse's brow.

Our Poesy is like that Gadarene
    Of old who roamed among the tombs, and raved,
And gashed himself with stones, and cried his
      threne
    To the sane Jesus, who rebuked and saved.
She, too, has come from out the burial-place,
    With night-voice by Minerva's owl depraved,
To meet the Wonder-Worker face to face
    And wait for Legion out of her to pass:
As they relinquish her from their embrace
    They rend her garments into Leaves of Grass.

The Wonder-Worker is our living truth—
    Truth of today, the knowledge of our age;
This shall restore old Poesy to youth,
    And bring her back to reason from her rage.
She shall look round herself and shall behold
    Religion, Story, Science on the stage
Of the new Learning's language, and grow bold
    To take her role with them and act her part;
Chief part, as in her glorious days of old,
    When she led nature captive to her art.

Yes, Poesy must play first character,
    Must queen it in this drama of the world,
Or else her singing-robes be stripped from her
    And she be in the ballet frocked and girled—

Her voice of goddess in the chorus drowned,
  Her gait of goddess capered, toed, and twirled.
Shall she be second? Where is first, then, found?
  In Music? Music is her serving-maid.
In Eloquence? When Eloquence is crowned
  He stands in her lent mantle of flame arrayed.

Painting and Sculpture rival for her hand;
  She is their sweetheart and their sovran. Yea,
All arts concenter on her, as a band
  Of damsels ringed around a Queen of May.
Yet she must wane away as moon no more,
  But orient herself and dawn as day.
The gods that she has practiced to adore,
  The liturgies employed to worship them,
The rhetoric defunct of fairy lore,
  Belong not to her New Jerusalem.

In this New City come down out of heaven,
  And given her to reign in if she will,
No pagan deities, as on the seven
  World-topping hills of Rome, the temples fill;
No satyrs, fauns, or nymphs there are to name
  And designate to wood, and vale, and hill;

It is old Nature newly searched with flame,
  Discovered newly by exploring mind—
The truth of things, the truth of words that aim
  The fine realities of things to find.

Words are her kingdom; Poetry is words;
  Words aptly chosen by their aptest sense,
But natural as babblement of birds;
  Words that are music, painting, eloquence;
That are keen light from out a core of fire,
  And are of things not seen soul's evidence;
That star the darkness of sublime desire
  With hintings of the somewhere-shining sun,
And chime our still thoughts like the morning-
      choir
  That sang together o'er creation done.

But Poesy must keep within the law;
  Her power of miracles is obsolete;
Plans of creation she anew must draw;
  Her miscreations she can ne'er complete;
Muse, Goddess, Triton, Siren, Fairy, Troll,
  Each a stark mummy in its winding-sheet,
She never shall re-word with life and soul.
  These are the names of fossils that belong
To mind of other epochs, and the whole
  Potence of life is gone from them in Song.

No! Song must throb in words of living speech;
　Must think the living thoughts of living men;
Must learn of living love what love can teach,
　And fire the world with living hope again;
Descend from ether to the atmosphere
　And breathe afresh the common oxygen.
Then wits no more shall query, with a sneer,
　How long may Poesy live after death.
She shall be known then, when she does appear,
　By this: She will not speak the Shibboleth.

THRENODY.

A gap is in our fireside-ring
  The wideness of a tiny tomb;
A prattle sweet as birds can sing
  Has left its hush in every room.

Our hearts long for the pretty charms
  Of babish questions manifold,
And for the little hugging arms
  Now locked across a bosom cold.

The bright hair and the eyes that beamed
  So wondrously, O how we miss!
And, O the loving lips! that seemed
  Fashioned so purposely to kiss.

As they who, yearning over sea,
  Grow homesick for their land and kin,
So we grow heaven-sick to be
  In that far land our love is in.

VICTRICE.

We walked where the grass was a checker
Of the light and the leaves of May,
When the Night in her white shroud of moonshine
Was the beautiful ghost of Day.

The presence that thrilled me with passion,
There under the moon and the shade,
Was a fond being, meek in her beauty,
Half seraph and half loving maid.

Her voice had the sorrowful cadence
Of winds of the night in the pine;
And her soul, like the mild moon of heaven,
Shone forth from her sad eyes to mine.

We had come unto where the world ended;
For out of the being of men
And into the bliss of angels
We had died and were born again.

Deep we drank of Love's river Lethéan,
  Till the moon in the west grew white
And along the gray shore of morning
  Broke the first purple billows of light.

As the inswelling floodtide of sunrise
  Rose over pale Lucifer's gleam,
She saw in the drowned star the symbol
  Of the end of our earthly dream.

She knew—and, O God! to remember
  How she told me this with her eyes!—
That she never again should behold me
  Till she met my soul in the skies.

O the pain and the passion of parting!
  For she knew that I needs must go,
Nor return till the year were dying
  And she lying under the snow.

O the pang and the anguish of parting!
  When she saw, and I could not see,
Saw the saraphim signaling to her,
  And her woman's-love hid it from me.

She loved me too dearly to slay me
  With the tidings her heart had heard;
And sadly she blessed me and kissed me,
  But said me no saddening word.

Sainted martyr of passion and victrice!
  How to memory now thou showst,
In love like the dying Redeemer,
  In peace like the Holy Ghost!

Didst thou hope I could bear it the better,
  Not to see thy beauty decline—
Not to have the gall and the wormwood
  Of memory mixed with the wine?

Bear it better! sweet sister of Jesus!
  When the sorrow of all the race,
The sorrow of loving and dying,
  I remember was in thy face!

O the shock and the fever of madness!
  When my soul, into darkness withdrawn,
Felt only those eyes in the moonlight,
  Saw only that face in the dawn!

But I came back to life and endured it;
  I said, I will bear my breath:
Surely, I should bear love and remembrance,
  Since she has borne love and death.

IN OBERON.

FRAGMENTS.

Conceive that hemisphere of Oberon,
Which is, as our own moon's, forever held
Faced to its planet by coincidence
Of motion axial with sidereal,
And that stupendous globe of Uranus,
Full seventy bulks of our earth massed in one
As viewed at distance of her satellite,
Hanging eternally in middle heaven,
And with its disk usurping half the sky.
The mighty orb looked neither sun nor moon;
But it is both; and with its light and heat,
Still saved within it since it was rolled off
From the expansed primeval solar fire,
It makes perpetual day, outsplendoring augnt
Seen, thought, or dreamed of tropic clime serene
In paradises of Pacific isles.
The great sphere bloomed in redness like a rose,
And from it to horizon down, the sky
Glowed as the sunsets Krakatoa once

Poured round and round our globe. The atmos-
  phere
Was as if melted ruby, and the breath of it
Was like the thrilling taste of rare old wine.

* * * * *

  Speech has the same use there that song has
    here;
It is a harp that sifts the airy thought;
Sweet speech, with no more reason there for being
Than verse has when it lilts through Kubla Khan
And fetches over into song divine
Far echoes of the meaning of a dream.

* * * * *

  Zoe was first to speak. No rare old violin,
With melody memorized in all its wood,
Singing its soul out in a master's hands—
No vox-humana of an organ-pipe
Sobbed solo down a great cathedral-aisle,
Lauding the Mother and the Son of God,
Could hint that marvelous voice to human sense;
Though it was low, it seemed to fill the world.
  13

ZOE.

My Zoen! Spirit of the Earth in thee!
Hast thou not now with me new interest
In that far world where thou and I have lived,
And have friends, kindred, and life's tender ties?
It seemed, when we were there in human flesh,
That births to misery and deaths in sin;
Pathetic suffrance under tragic wrong;
Meek innocence upon the shameful cross;
Red glut of murder on the battlefield;
Crusading slaughter in the name of Christ,
His footsteps bloodied from the sacred ground
Under fierce Islam's banner of the moon;
The game of lions played with mangled limbs
Of Christian girls to sport the bloody shes
Who mothered heroes in old pagan Rome;
The hells of martyrdom (the hells on earth
To propagate the faith that Hell awaits
Beyond); man's brutal bondage, making brutes
Of slave and master both; the servitude
Of toil to syndicates of robbery;
The deadly competitions of grim want
With fatted greed; the littered swarms
Of population, heirs of lust and crime,
Squandered in famine, pestilence, and war—

It seemed to us that such enormities
Of sorrow, sin, disease, and cruel death
Were heritages of a primal curse,
Foul stains upon the nature of the world,
And that the hope of an escape therefrom
By being pardoned into Paradise
Was all the solace that remained to man.
But here, my Zoen, we have clearer light.
We see no foredesign of special fate
For any world, no supernatural scheme
For singling one world from the universe
Of worlds to damn it wholly at the first
And save it partly afterward.

ZOEN.

No, love;
As we remember through to origin
The course of life in our world Oberon,
We recognize the Omnipresent Mind
(We know not what it is, for, as mere parts
Thereof, we can not comprehend the whole,
But of it only dream and name it God)
Thinking in terms of matter—chaos first,
Then lumps of worlds, instinct with energies
And potencies, from which spring forms of life,

Which are God's forms of thought; low forms **at**
    start,
But growing higher, as the Thinking grows
In clearness, till at length the highest forms
Take memory of all their own world's past,
Take all that world's life into consciousness,
To make it God's complete idea there.

ZOE.

How, then, do we explain the evil of the
    Earth—
Such evil as we know we have outgrown
In Oberon—if God is conscious good?

ZOEN.

We argue from a premise undefined
And predicate of what we do not know
When we essay to deal with attributes
That faith ascribes to God. Omnipotence,
Omniscience, and Benevolence Divine
Assembled in a Person are not God.
What is omnipotence but all the powers
Of all the universe together summed?
What is omniscience but the total mind
Evolved to consciousness in all degrees
On all the peopled worlds flocked round the suns?

And is not that divine benevolence
Which, blocking out the globes from chaos, builds,
Through forces ever feeling toward the good,
Worlds orderly and beautiful as this?

ZOE.

There are in Earth who reason that, if God
Created matter and if evil comes
From this, then evil has its origin
In him as its first cause. Discourse of that.

ZOEN.

We know as little as they know on Earth
What matter in itself or what God is;
But this we know, that neither they nor we
Have faculties to fancy or to dream,
Much less to think, that something has begun
From nothing or in nothing can have end.
Matter's beginning is unthinkable;
And, since we cannot think it, matter has,
For our mind, no beginning; matter is,
As God is, uncreated and eternal.
What we term evil, then, is foreordained
No more than cosmic gravitation is.
We see the force which holds the worlds together

Seize him who topples from a tower's hight
And hurtle him to death against the ground.
Would we annul the law of gravity
And let star-systems tumble all apart
To save from downfall that small mass of life?
No less is gravity a part of God
Than is benevolence. Almighty power
Must function through its organs—can not make
Its gravitation merciful to sin
Or pitiful to pain.

ZOE.

What, then, is sin,
That it estops divine benevolence,
And that omnipotence must arm itself
Against it with the vengeful sword of pain?

ZOEN.

Sin is the struggle of the partial wills
Of matter with the Universal Will
Of Mind—the nature (Spirit to be born)
Of things contending to possess themselves
Of the estate of life and living soul.
Sin educates. Sin teaches mind the laws
Of matter by the test of penalties.

Hence every sin is sworded round with pain.
We can not reason wherefore pain should be;
But can we wherefore pleasure should? On Earth
The lands and seas are populous with lives
Devouring one another for their food;
And pain of life devoured must be, no less
Than pleasure of the life devouring is,
An incident of progress into higher life;
Wherein, as here, we recollect the twain
As warp and woof of finished web of bliss.

ZOE.

But shall the life of Earth develop there,
Evolving evil out, evolving death,
Till mankind take, as we of Oberon,
A common consciousness of all their world,
Inherit memory of all its dead,
And live them over in immortal youth?

ZOEN.

However much we of the past may know,
We can but hope the future. Worlds there are,
Doubtless, that fail of consummation's flower,
As earth's dead moon, whose life is gathered up,
Or shall be, in remembrance otherwhere;

But earth's conditions promise permanence
To her warm zone for millions of her years;
And there, I doubt not, shall the race of man
Ascend to altitudes of being, dreams
Of mortal would not dare to prophesy.
Though it can never have as high a form
As evolution has created here
(Earth's greater gravity forbade the wings),
Yet it shall so complete the form it has,
So by invention aid and supplement,
That it shall master all the elements
And dominate the forces of the world.
If light and heat endure upon that planet
Till time has brought fulfillment of the laws
Of fit survival and heredity
Of apt selection—apter ruled by thought—
Man shall no longer pine for future Heaven,
But live more heaven than all his past has dreamed.

ZOE.

Yet, O! the long, long ages it will need
To breed the tiger out of human life,
To slack the poison-serpent's wicked coil,
The grapple of the hideous devil-fish,
The mobbing rush of wolfish ravinings!
O peaceful lands to bleed with havoc yet!

O seas to smoke with battle's thunder-guns!
O women! who shall wail the centuries full
Of curses on the scrofulous Blue Blood
Whose armed insaneness and ensoldiered hate
Shall still disman and desolate your homes.
The willing laborer shall hunt for toil
While his wan wife and puny children wait
In famine for his wage. The carpenter
Of Nazareth shall still be put to shame
By Christian Divès spurning from his door
The Jesus-blessèd, or delivering them
To Christian jails for guilt of going hungry.
Love's wrecks of chastity shall walk the streets
By night—God! O just God! hast thou no whip
Of lightning, zigzag with almighty wrath,
To lash these brute wrongs headlong down to hell?

ZOEN.

This is access of human passion. Think
No longer now of Earth's diseases; think
Now only of the splendid bloom of life
That is to issue from the sodden saps
Of sin which ooze up from we know not where,
And grow from darkness and blow into day.
We have not searched the secrets of the night,
But we do know the signs of dawn. We know,

From conscious history of Oberon,
Brought through all glooms yon Earth is passing
    through,
That life is rising to its morning there.
Science is catching up the light of it
Along her warming mountain-tops of snow;
Its glow creeps down the slopes; begins to flush
The fogs and stirring shadows of the vales.
Commerce shall flock the waters with the wings
Of sailing Peace—the steel-mailed hulks of War
Oozed in among old bones of Viking-ships
At the dead bottom of unsounded seas.
Carousing hurricanes that madly dance
The ocean-floors shall be controlled to sane
Tame powers pushing in obedience
To navigation, and the skill of man
Shall take the wild waves by their tossing manes
And stroke them into gentle servitors
To bear him dangerless from shore to shore.
So merchandry shall freely ebb and flow
About the globe and mix together minds,
And languages, and races, till, at last,
One race, one language, one consense of mind,
Shall integrate humanity. The weight
Of that dense planet pulling from the sun
Makes problems of aerial waftage hard—
Too hard for evolution to have solved

For highest life—yet sometime intellect
Shall work the miracle, ingrafting wings
Upon dead matter, breathing into it
Force as a living soul, and riding it,
As if an emmet on an eagle's back,
Along the lofty highways of the winds.
The energies of nature, heat, and light,
And electricity (or what names else—
They all are one), born servants to the force
Named life, shall be enskilled to do its work,
Lifting all burdens from the neck of toil,
As here, and leaving mind, the master, time
To star itself amid sky-silences,
To prick the canopy of mystery through
And sift-down glory from the upper flame.

ISLE-OF-WILLOWS.

A little bird with a scarlet coat
Came fluting to me a silvery note,
As though it said through its mellow throat,
  Isle-of-Willows! Isle-of-Willows!

It perched alone on a lonely tree,
And seemed that it longed and longed to be
In the isle it sung of thus to me,
  Isle-of-Willows! Isle-of-Willows!

It thought perhaps of a little islé
Where blue the waters and heavens smile
'And green the willows wave all the while—
  Isle-of-Willows! Isle-of-Willows!

Is this thy memory or thy hope—
Thy being's backward or forward scope,
Whereto thy little heart-longings grope?—
  Isle-of-Willows! Isle-of-Willows!

It said me never another word,
But flitted away, this little bird;
Yet aye in my soul its voice is heard—
  Isle-of-Willows! Isle-of-Willows!

THE AMERICAN CITIZEN.

No scutcheon I have to be blazoned by,
No *von* or *de* for a family-tie
 To a pomp of grandfathers eight or ten;
I was not born in the purple, but I
 Am a born American Citizen.

No lordship incarnates itself in me
Through blood newly blued by a royal decree
 Or filtered of old from a prince of men,
But an honor I boast of higher degree—
 I am an American Citizen.

Nobility out of the veins of the dead
Belongs to the past; the present, instead,
 Makes manhood the measure of man again,
And chooses blood that is livingly red
 To make the American Citizen.

As once it was in the glorious day
When Rome was queen of the world in her sway,
 Romanus sum was the proudest claim then,
So in that old Roman spirit I say,
 I am an American Citizen.

The pride of the Great Republic I bear;
I feel her majesty move in the air,
  Her greatness to come and her glory when
A thousand million of freemen shall share
  The name of American Citizen.

Behold her ruling the world of the West,
Her rule of the most the rule of the best,
  When the brave man's voice, and the true man's
    pen,
And the free man's vote have wholly possessed
  The future American Citizen.

I pray that her strength and grandeur increase
To tutor the world in the ways of peace,
  Till the lamb shall lie in the lion's den
And the wars of Kings at the bidding cease
  Of the strong American Citizen.

O, I hail her flag with the stars bedight,
I see her power for freedom and right,
  I thrill with her power beyond my ken,
As I feel that the coming man in his might
  Shall be the American Citizen.

MADONNA.

Hail, O Madonna! my woman, my lady!
  Mine by my poesy, mine by my dreams!
Not as a nymph of the leafily shady
    Myth of the wilderness, nor as the limbs
    Nude of a naiad in fountains and streams
      Glimpsed as she flashes, and plashes, and swims,
But as a real live woman, Madonna!

Future-forefeeling old poets, then seeing
  Nowhere in all the world lady like mine,
Feigned an ideal aerial being,
    Oread or dryad, that, piped to by Pan,
    Danced in the solitudes, where the divine
      Passion of beauty has visited man
Always in guise of my woman, Madonna!

Or the delicious keen charm of illusion
  (Rapturous chase of the soul after sense)
Fabled they, dreaming the plunge and the fusion
    Into clear waters of womanly shapes;
    Bosoms that hid in the crystal defense,
      Bodies that made hurried bashful escapes
Into the fountains, revealed thee, Madonna!

Thou art the mystery, thou art the beauty,
    Left to the world from the world's age of gold;
Thou art the thought holding heroes to duty;
    Thou art that secret in music and rhyme
    Which has been guessed at, but never been told;
    Thou art the dreamed-of and longed-for of
      time,
Glory of womanhood, lady Madonna!

THE LAND REDEEMED.

Not always shall the good earth be
  To man's use under ban ;
The land shall be redeemed at last
  And rendered back to man ;
Then each shall of the acres hold
  Enough to make him free ;
None shall usurp more than his need,
  And none shall landless be.

The system of old feudal wrong
  That makes the people pay
For room to live upon the earth
  Shall fade and fall away ;
The name of landlord shall become
  A mockery and scoff,
As rolls the tide of human rights
  To sweep his landmarks off.

For man shall yet perceive the truth—
  Through old tradition dim—
That record, scroll, nor parchment writ
  Can take the earth from him ;
14

That nature makes a title-deed
  To each one for his time
In his own want, and who takes more
  He perpetrates a crime.

This living truth shall flush the cheek
  Of pale Starvation red,
As over old ancestral parks
  The pauper's sheaves are spread;
This truth shall wrest from blood and birth
  The scepter and the crown,
And, leveling the Workers up,
  The Drones shall level down.

Then prince and peasant side by side
  Shall strive, with heart and brain,
By doing highest work for man
  The highest rank to gain;
For, when each has his human right
  Of home upon the soil,
The Worker shall be prince and king—
  God's Nobleman of Toil!

Glad time of earth's beatitude!
  When none shall hoard or steal,
But all mankind together work
  For universal weal;

When war no more shall shock the land
  Or thunder on the sea,
But by the Golden Rule of Christ
  All wrongs shall righted be.

DUTY HERE AND GLORY THERE.

Darkness that my heart could feel of,
Blackness that my soul could swim in,
Drowned in me the living spirit,
   Strength to hope and will to dare;
Murder-shrieks that shock the midnight,
And that pierce, and pang, and sicken,
Would have brought me grateful respite
   From that death, that death despair;
When a preternatural whisper—
Words that sounded not, but touched me—
Seemed to utter through me to me,
   'Duty here and glory there!'

Where? My soul looked round and questioned;
Boom of thunder-throated cannon,
Clash of steel, and clang of music
   Strove in vain to answer where.
Then loud senatorial voices,
Stormy with a people's passion,
Swollen with a nation's power,
   Seemed grand answers in the air.
But the cannon, and the clashing,

And the music, and the voices
Never echoed to that whisper,
  'Duty here and glory there!'

Showers of delicious praises,
Falling on the panting spirit
Like the cooling rains of summer,
  Cherishing great souls that bear
Thought's immortal bloom of beauty
Wafting round the world the fragrance
Of their names—Ambition questioned,
  'Worth not these the weary wear,
Through a lifelong toil and patience,
Wear of soul and wear of body?'
No response in that felt whisper,
  'Duty here and glory there!'

Where? My soul looked up and questioned—
Up to where the stars were burning
In the grand and awful temple
  Of the midnight—up to where
Vision stops against the curtain
Of the infinite, but spirit
Puts aside the vail and enters;
  It is there! O, it is there!
Thrilled the whisper through my being,
'Duty here for little lifetimes,
Glory there for endless ages—
  Duty here and glory there!'

REMEMBER THE MAINE.

Americans, can you forget our ship Maine?
How she went to her grave in the fetid flood,
A coffin for thirteenscore men of our blood,
In a dynamite hell of murder by Spain?
No! remember the Maine and—remember Spain!

We forget not her history's bloody stain
On the map of the world, her wars west and east,
Her sign of the Cross always mark of the Beast;
But we have an affair of our own with Spain:
We remember the Maine and—remember Spain!

Two hundred and sixtysix men of the Maine
Done to death in their sleep is an 'incident'
For diplomacy, is it, Sir President?
O take not, my People, blood-money from Spain,
But remember the Maine and—remember Spain!

Shall six hundred thousand appeal in vain
From their graves of starvation in Cuba's Isle,
While we with palaver and Christianly smile
Plead for Wall-street peace and the credit of Spain!
No! remember the Maine and—remember Spain!

The Nation is one, and our duty is plain:
  We owe it to justice, we owe it to law
  Of the nations, the vengeful swift sword to draw
And wave it for thunder of guns upon Spain—
To remember the Maine and—remember Spain!

Let our ships flock forth on the old Spanish Main,
  Let our guns blast her out of her islands here,
  Till her flag's last hold in the hemisphere
We capture for freedom, for freedom from Spain,
And remember the Maine on the seas with Spain!

April, 1898.

THE THOUGHT AND THE WORD.

My thought is a soaring eagle,
My word a serpent on the ground:
    The serpent crawls,
    The eagle falls
Swifter than sight or sound.

A grapple of steely talons,
    A grip of coiling fetters round;
    And up the skies
    The eagle flies,
Eagle with serpent bound.

A fight in the open heaven,
    And round and downward settling slow
    The strong bird sinks—
    With snaky links
Throttled to death below.

A curse on the strangling serpent!
    O that my eagle did but know
    How down to stoop
    And with one swoop
Finish him at a blow!

LOVE IN THE SUGAR-CAMP.

What sweeter of the sweets of youth—
Of youth abloom and springtime sunny—
   Than love's night in the sugar-booth
Round kettles of the maple honey?

   All day the live trees have distilled
From thawy mold their luscious juices,
   And all day down the spiles has rilled
The nectar from the barky sluices.

   The grove's run, twice collected in,
Has kept all day the caldrons fuming,
   And now their winy foams begin
To sirup into golden spuming.

   Swains come with sweethearts from the farms—
The farm's young men and maidens pairing—
   Along lone paths, where moonrise charms
Their steps to linger, hither faring.

   As flock the couples to the glow,
Just where the shine with shadow closes
   Hearts peep from eyes and blushes blow
Out of the dark like morning roses.

All one another greet by name
(There are no Misters and no Misses),
    And girls touch boyish lips with flame
By proxy of their mutual kisses.

    They sing old songs, they play old plays,
They run the revels of old dances,
    And make the hours between the days
Realities of old romances.

    And now they huddle to the board
(The dear so near that pulses quicken),
    Where into earthen trays is poured
The bubbling mell to cool and thicken.

    The damsels knead the waxen cakes,
And shape them for the banquet handy,
    And that night many a fond pair makes
The tie that binds of ropes of candy.

    O cheeks of roses, hair of flax,
And eyes like heaven in April weather,
    My dream still tastes that maple wax
And that sweet love of you together.

.

Ah! rarer than the work of bees,
Ah! finer than love's later fashion,
The sweetness from the sugar-trees,
The sweetness of the heart's first passion!

ASPIRATION AND INSPIRATION.

We weary waiting for these glimmerings
Which struggle singly through the difficult rifts
Of aspiration from the overworld.
O for some breezy circumstance at once
To take the cloud off from our starry thoughts
And let their glory constellate the dark!
The spirit's brightest outgrowths are of pain,
As precious pearls are of disease in shells
At bottom of the deep. The slow, obscure,
Still process of the rain, distilling down
The great sweat of the sea, is never seen
In the consummate spectacle flashed forth
A seven-hued arch upon the clouds of heaven:
So never sees the world those energies,
Stern effort and long patience, which have stirred
In toil's humility and slowly heaved
Its darkness up, till sudden glory springs
Forth on it, showing like the spanning rainbow.
   Think ye the lofty foreheads of the world,
Which shine as full moons through the night of
       time,

Holding their calm big splendor steadily
Forever at the top of history,
Think ye they rushed up with the suddenness
Of rockets aimlessly shot into heaven,
And flared to their eternal places there?
The vulgar years through which ambition gropes,
Reaching and feeling for its destiny,
Are only years of chaos, tallied not
On the memorial rocks, but covered deep
Under the stratified history of a world.
   Celebrity by some great accident,
Some single opportunity, is like
Aladdin's palace in the Arabian tale,
Vanished when envy steals the wizard's charm.
But thought up-pyramids itself to fame
By husbandry of opportunities,
Grade upon grade constructing, till its hight,
Descried above time's far horizon, slopes
With peak among the stars. Go mummify
Thy name within that architectural pile
Another's intellect has builded; none—
For all the hieroglyphs of glory—none
Save but the builder's name shall signify
To the remembering ages.
                  Heart and brain
Of thine need resolutely yoke themselves

To slow-paced years of toil—need feel and think
(A bibulous memory sponging up the thoughts
Of dead men is not thought)—else all the trumps
Of hero-heraldry that ever twanged,
Gathered in one mad blare above the graves,
Shall not avail to resurrect thy name
To the salvation of remembrance then
When once the letters of it have slunk back
Into the alphabet from off thy tomb.
Ay, think or perish! Marble frets and crumbles
Down into undistinguishable dust
At last, and epitaphs grooved into brass
Yield piecemeal to the hungry elements;
But thoughts that drop plumb to the depths of truth
Anchor the name forever and forever.

INNERVALE.

At the base of a marvelous mountain,
  Whose hights human foot never trod,
There gushes a crystalline fountain
  And makes a bright brook in the sod.

And the sod greens away o'er a valley
  That opens where blue waters be;
And the brook with meandering dally
  Goes babbling along to the sea.

There, snowy sails pass like the lazy
  White clouds of a summer-blue sky—
Appear and evanish where hazy
  Infinity fences the eye.

Here, asleep upon Pan's mossy pillows—
  By Pan piped asleep in these groves,—
Dreaming Poesy hears the low billows
  Breeze-babbled from echoing coves.

And here, while the leaves sift the sunny
  Swift sands of the day from above,
The wild-bee gads hunting for honey,
  With wings wove of whispers of love.

Here the ripples make music like olden
  Weird monotones thrummed on a lute;
Here the dark skies of green are starred golden
  With thick constellations of fruit.

In this valley, alone but not lonely,
  Beside where the brook-waters run,
Stands one little cottage, one only,
  Dwells one little maid, only one.

Her blue eyes are clear pools of passion,
  Her lips have the tremor of leaves,
And the speech that her loving thoughts fashion
  Is sweeter than poetry weaves.

Though the vale is by sleep so surrounded
  That her ne'er a wooer shall win,
On the side by the sea of dreams bounded
  With her I sail out and sail in.

SHIPS COMING IN.

I lay upon a rock that jutted to the sea.
Twilight came down from out the pine-woods back
  of me,
And, stealing on the waters, met the sudden moon,
Rushed into her kiss, and sank to a dead white
  swoon.
I lay there on the rock and thought of all had been,
I lay and watched my ships come in, my ships come
  in.

Sail, O ships! my home-voyaging ships!
  Sail from the sunlit side of the world;
    Climb the watery bulge of the globe;
Pass the line where the orient dips
  In the sea, and, with canvas unfurled,
    Take yon moon's glory on as a robe:
From wherever your sailing has been,
Sail, ships, hither, sail hither, sail in.

Ship! that flew out of port with thy wings
  Dipt in morning, is yon phantom thou—
    Moonlit phantom that drifts to the strand
And no freight and no passenger brings?
15

Yet see! one there alive on the prow,
   In his gaze the sick hunger for land:
Hope! my Captain! that sailed out to win
All our world—conquered Captain, sail in.

Ship! that pushed to the tropical zone,
   Touched spice-islands in summery seas,
     Then, in mad equatorial gales,
Went adrift with one mariner lone—
   Bring him back from the sunned Caribbees,
     Bring him in with thy storm-tattered sails:
Love! my Sailor! once life's happy twin,
Now sweet ghost of life, specter! sail in.

Ship! that steered for the boreal stars,
   And, bewitched by the weird northern-lights,
     Cramped through ice-packs and wintered in
     snows
Heaped to the deck and piled to the spars,
   Thou hast brought from the long arctic nights
     Only one, and him famished and froze;
Fame! my Helmsman! Anatomy thin
Propt to the wheel, stark Helmsman, sail in.

Ship! that went out to traffic with Ind,
  Hugged the Gold Coast, and doubled Good
    Hope,
    When full sail on the Asian sea,
Thou wast caught by a contrary wind
  And blown down the world's southerly slope
    And thence upward and hither to me:
Ship, whose lading did never begin,
With this moonshine for cargo! sail in.

Ship! that searched round the world for new lands,
  Sounded new seas and charted new skies,
    Studied new stars, new sights of the sun,
Then plowed keel in the ooze and the sands—
  There in shallows thy mystery lies,
    When all the deeps thy sailing has done:
Psyche wove but the Parcae did spin
Warp and woof of thy sail sailing in.

Ship! that struck the horizon's sea-line
  And there vanished away in the blue,
    Seemed that thy sail went into the sky,
And not down the east ocean's decline:
  Is naught, then, but the underworld true,
    And yon overworld naught but a lie?
Faith! my Anchor! all rusted with sin,
There on deck of this ship sailing in!

ALONE.

Alone! alone!
Forth out of the darkness,
Back into the darkness,
  We come and we go alone.

O birth! O death!
Lone cry from the midnight,
Moan lost in the midnight,
  A catch and a lapse of breath!

O youth! fleet dream!
We sleep out of heaven,
We dream down from heaven,
  Then wake from the fleeting dream.

No more! no more!
Youth's gladness of living,
Love's madness of living,
  Can come back to me no more.

Those glad, mad years!
How, dancing and singing,
How danced and went winging
  Those passionate choral years!

To be! to live!
What being, what living,
What largess of living
  The blood of the boy can give!

O earth! O heaven!
Earth glad with all beauty,
And no hint of duty
  From all the glad blue of heaven!

Sun, moon, and stars!
Lakes, woods with birds flying
Through them, and the crying
  Of insects beneath the stars!

Then life in love!
Life's torrent-stream steadied,
Stopt, flowed back, and eddied
  About in the pool of love.

From boy to man!
Bridge built of a rainbow—
Love's luminous rainbow,
  Which fadeth from boy to man.

Love's fading bow !
Still following hither,
I follow on whither
  It lures me and I must go.

Yes, follow on !
Love's rainbow-ideal,
So nigh and so real,
  Still flies, but I follow on.

For love is all !
Hope, pleasure, ambition,
Fame's fullest fruition,
  Are nothing ; for love is all.

But age grows lone !
For age is unlovely—
Age wins not the lovely ;—
  We go as we came, alone.

Alone ! alone !
Forth out of the darkness,
Back into the darkness,
  We come and we go alone.

NEARING THE BRINK.

Now steady, old heart—we are nearing the brink!
  Let us front our fate boldly: we can not face back;
  For the Hours are mad wolves in full chase on our
    track
From the steppes to the sea, and the moment we
    shrink
  The whole swift tumultuous ravinous pack
Will scuffle us, hustle us over the brink.

A minute to think—but a minute ere doom—
  Of the high meadows back in their beauty of
    spring,
  Of the bright brooks aflow and the songbirds
    a-wing,
Of the blue skies aglow and the green plains
    abloom—
  Now wide wastes of snow to the vision's far ring,
The pack at our heels, and a minute to doom!

One rush, then the plunge and the drop to the sea—
  Hear the surge at the foot of the precipice roar!
  O! the leap from the land's-end—to sink or to
    soar?

If the quick and the dead shall divide you and me,
    Old heart, we must part as we take the leap o'er,
I sunward to soar, you to sink in the sea.

And yet, my old heart, there is no other way.
    All the seasons of joyance are past long ago:
    Spring and summer and autumn are under the
        snow,
And the hungry horizons, a-swarm for their prey,
    From east, west, and north now are closing in so
That all there is left us is this only way.

The Hours, the lean Hours, the keen Hours huddle
        in.
    They have tasted the blood in our tracks on the
        waste,
    And our life is a forfeit to that eager taste:
Though we halt or go headlong, they win, they will
        win;
    For we are their prey, if devoured or effaced,
Their prey or their triumph, as they huddle in.

The scars of life's mad and sad passions on you,
    Wounded heart, shall be drowned all away in the
        deep;

Unto you shall be rest, unto you shall be sleep;
But for me—if to wake and, with memory true,
   To take all our past, all your sorrows—the leap!
With you, dear old heart, to the darkness with you!

THE END.

www.ingramcontent.com/pod-product-compliance
Lightning Source LLC
Chambersburg PA
CBHW020113030726

47498CB00006B/2080